Jean Buffong is a Grenadian who has lived in England since 1962. Her novella, *Jump-Up-And-Kiss-Me*, was published together with Nellie Payne's *A Grenadian Childhood* in the popular *Jump-Up-And-Kiss-Me: Two Stories From Grenada* (The Women's Press, 1990). *Under the Silk Cotton Tree* is her long-awaited first full-length novel.

To

Jennifer.

Love.

Buffong.

21/7/95

Also by Jean Buffong, with Nellie Payne and introduced by
Merle Collins, published by The Women's Press:

Jump-Up-And-Kiss-Me: Two Stories From Grenada (1990).

Under the
Silk Cotton Tree

JEAN BUFFONG

A NOVEL

First published by The Women's Press Ltd 1992
A member of the Namara Group
34 Great Sutton Street, London EC1V 0DX

British Library Cataloguing in Publication Data
A catalogue record for this book is available from the British
Library

ISBN 0 7043 4317 7

Phototypeset by Intype
Printed and bound in Great Britain by
BPCC Hazells Ltd
Member of BPCC Ltd.

To my mother for nurturing me and to aunty Agnes and cousin Ann who have helped rekindle our dying flame of storytelling.

1

I have never heard anything like it in all my life – never. If teacher Marion knew the old lady would of carried on like that she would not of invited her to the church. Then again the lady is really stubborn, you know. If they tried to get her to stay in the house with the food and things she might start quarrelling and saying it's because people don't like her. They jealous because her granddaughter getting married. I don't know . . . everything nice and peaceful then, just like that it sounded like the devil himself was in the church. The priest . . . you should of seen his face. I was right in front, so I was able to see everything. I made sure I had a front pew because it was the first time that I been to a proper wedding, so I didn't want to miss anything. I don't mean that I never been to a wedding like, but was the first time I been in the choir and able to see what really went on at the altar. The priest was busy busy performing the service . . . said some prayers and things. Said some nice things about the two teachers. That didn't surprise me really, because they were two of the nicest teachers the school ever had. Well, the priest did all his business and just as he got to the most serious part, then things happened. As he started 'I now pronounced you man and . . . ' he didn't finished. One

'O Gawd, Lawd have mercy' broke out in the church. 'Lawd have mercy Am way bacay oye me belly me belly O Gawd'; well I tell you, even now it's hard to describe the atmosphere in the church at that time. The priest looked up, his colour changed as if all the ashes on Ash Wednesday fell on him. I tell you it was the loudest screech, not just loudest but funny like, as if it was not from a real person it came. That was the funniest thing I heard since Aunt Sar died and Tanty Mildred hollowed out when she realised that her sister dead . . . really gone for good.

I can hear the sound in my head after all that time. Sort of deep deep down in my head I can hear the bawling. Sometimes I think I have special hole in my head storing up all these things. At the time Aunt Sar died we were accustomed to when people died to hear others bawling all kind of papa bunjay oye and saying all kind of things. Sometimes as if they confessing all their deeds, perhaps hoping that the dead person would forgive them, but this time was something else.

We knew the lady was old and expect her to die anytime. I mean me, Fatima and my cousin Verna, although we were little, yet we were accustomed to death, you know, not because our family always dying but if there is a death in the village every body was around helping and thing. So when Aunt Sar died it was nothing to us. We practically lived with the three women, even when Uncle JJ was living there. They had no children, so all the children in the village were theirs.

As I was saying, as children we were not afraid at all. We were in and out of the room where she was laid out on the bed ready to be bathe, dressed and put in the coffin. She laid on the bed flat on her back like if she was sleeping, but we knew she was dead because for one thing she never slept on

2

her back and the other she was too quiet. She always tossing about and talking as if she and somebody fighting. Anyway, to us children she was old and died. We were sad and cried a little, but to begin with we were more interested in the rice tea and saltfish souse during the wake. Tanty Avis and Tanty Mildred, well, that was something else. At one time I was afraid for them; worried that they would fall down and die as well. Although they were old that would still of been a lot of trouble. When they started holding their belly and falling down all over the place, that was really scary. Tanty Mildred seemed to be in another world. These two women bawled and bawled. I don't know where they got the eye-water from. They moaned from the time Aunt Sar died right up to the eight days' prayers, and even after that was as if they went funny in the head. The night of the eight-day prayer Tanty Avis got a hammer and started pounding the house, saying she mashing down the damn place because the house too big for them now. After a while things started to settle down, people just carried on, but as I said it was not the same for the two old sisters. I supposed in a way was just as when Janice died. It's been a long time now, but sometimes it's just like yesterday.

Even now sometimes, Mammy look at me as if her eyes screaming at me. I used to think that she blamed me for Janice death. To tell the truth when she first died I used to prayer to God to forgive me, because I used to think it was my fault that my little sister died just like that. Just so.

We shared a bedroom. Had one big bed. Sometimes we used to fight to sleep in front the bed away from under the window in case spirit came in on us in the night, especially after the time Mammy got up with a big round purple mark on her leg. She said was a pipe mark. It was just like the

3

mark that my friend Sonia mother had on her arm a few weeks before. According to Sonia, her mother said that was Mr Joshua who used to lived in the pasture that put it there. I didn't know how she could say a thing like that, especially as the man was her godfather. The man looked harmless, he can't even slap mosquito biting him, but according to Sonia he was the biggest lougarou in the place. Me, I don't know. To me if anybody making nastiness is Miss O'Brien that living in the little house next to Mr Joshua. That woman is something else. Everybody 'fraid of her.

One day, me and Sheila was going up Cacoben Hill; sun hot for so. When we reached by Miss Eva house one strap of my slipper burst. It was a bit dry rot anyway, so as if the hot sun finished it off. Well the pitch hot like fire, the bush on the side of the road just as hot, I can't walk with only side of slipper on my foot. Sheila said Caryle, that's Miss Eva son, does repair shoes so he wouldn't mind tacking the strap for me. We stood in the gap and called Caryle. We called and called but no answer, but we heard as if there were people talking on the bottom side of the house down by the sea. To be honest I don't know why Miss Eva built her house on this precipice. If another hurricane Janet pass, before the wind start to blow, she and her family end up straight out in the ocean. People say when she wanted to build the house she had a lot of problems getting carpenters to help her. Nobody wanted to work on that precipice. Not only how the piece of land bad, but they said Jasper used to meet the devil under the gru-gru tree over the road and sometimes under the big tambranch tree. Some people say they meet him up in all different ways around there in the middle of the night.

I think was two years ago, one thing broke out. Nobody

4

really knew what really happened. Was around harvest time. The Catholic always make their harvest in the big school, and then have a big dance in the night. Anyway, was after midnight when Reynold and a set of boys were coming home from the dance they saw this thing. They said as soon as they turned the corner coming towards the gru-gru tree they saw a shadow. Some of them said it looked like a beast, some said it was only a shadow. They were not sure because it happened so quickly. Only Carlton said it was a naked man; these boys lie so much you don't know what to believe. What was for sure was something left from under the gru-gru tree made one dash across the road; when it reached on the spot where Miss Eva house is now, it stopped, looked at the boys, then threw itself down the precipice. They said everything happened so quickly, nobody had a chance to say a word. Was as if they turned to stone, until Carlton let out one piece of 'O Gawd bunjay oye', and by the time they catch themselves only his white pants foot they saw pounding the road in the darkness. When Carlton reached his mother house, he gave the door one boaw doaw boaw and pelt inside. His parents jumped out of bed. All ask his father, asking, 'What's wrong?' He can't answer. His eyes popping out of his head, his tongue rolling about in his mouth. Same time his mother got the bottle of bay rum mixed with cacajab and started rubbing him down.

Aye aye one bacanal in the place the next morning. Some people said it was jumbie going home. They reckon the jumbie lived in the silk cotton tree by the side of the tam-branch tree. They say it could be because Carlton disturbed it, that why it wanted to turn the boy into a dummy. Others said it was Jasper doing his nastiness, and he wanted to make sure they don't talk. People always said that man does turn into all kind of things, even wedding cake. I don't know how human being could turn into beast and wedding cake to dance in the road in the middle of the night, but in this Grenada the more you live the more you hear. Whatever it was, from that night everybody was afraid to walk up the hill. When we went to school we used to walk fast fast. About a year after that Miss Eva built her house there. It was a good thing, though, because we were not afraid to walk up there anymore. Anyway, as I was saying, me and Sheila stood in the gap calling Caryle, hoping he would sew up the slipper for me. We couldn't hear any sound in the house but there was a sort of noise, a sort of mmmmmm mmmmmm coming from behind the house nearer to the sea. It sounded like two persons talking but not using proper words like . . . a kind of mmmmmm from one person and a sw . . . ish swiiiiish from the other. Sheila such a coward she started pulling my skirt for us to leave, but the pitch burning under my foot like fire so I wanted the slipper fixed.

I kept on calling Caryle, at the same time moving a few steps in the yard to peep round the back of the house down by the sea. Well; this time I was the one ready to run. I couldn't believe my eyes; the woman was standing on the big stone in the sea. She was lucky the sea wasn't rough. Everybody was afraid of Miss O'Brien; is now I understand why. She was wearing a long black dress and a nylon black headtie. She had her arms over her head, her eyes staring straight up to the sky as if she talking to God. The 'voices' we heard was her and the waves. She was there as if pleading with God, or perhaps asking Him to put curse on somebody. I'm sure it wasn't God she was talking to, though. I always heard people saying that the woman hand is never clean, now I understand what they meant.

The way she stood out in the sea reminded of the time the river took Miss Sagoo. That is something I would never forget until they put me six feet under. To see how me and Sheila shouted to the woman to come out of the river; shouted to her that the river coming down. Shout; bawling to her you know, before she even looked at us. She didn't believe us at first, because no rain fell at all that day. Rain didn't even set up, the mountain was bright bright. The sun having hot gossip with the ground, like the usual Lenten season. Some places so dry not one green leaf on any tree, just parched . . . brown dry. Some of the trees so naked you could see clear clear from one place to the other. When I stand up on the big stone behind the kitchen, I see the big boucanoe tree way up in Mr Touse land up Mt. Plaisir. The day the river take Miss Sagoo, me and Sheila was in the river washing. We didn't have rain to study, then all of a sudden the water started to look kind of dirty dirty. I say all of a sudden because it was as if we dipped the clothes in clean water, lift it out of dirty water.

Sheila first noticed it; not how it was dirty but how the water was getting deeper. She was in the deep water hole bathing when she shouted to me. I heard Sheila saying something, but I did not pay attention to her. I heard her shouting but kept on scrubbing under Mammy working dress arm with a corn stick.

'Flora,' she said. 'Flora, listen. Hear that tumbaying up Mt. Plaisir. It look as if the river coming down!'

'What you mean river coming down?' I said. 'You always with your stupidness. You ever see river come down without rain fall? Perhaps is blast they blasting up in the hills.' While I talking I dipped the dress in the water to rinse it out; it was then I noticed the colour of the water. Not only the colour but I realise the water was reaching up to my shin.

'Bonjay Sheila,' I shouted. 'The water look dirty!'

'Jesus Christ. I see what you mean. It look as if the river coming down. The water coming up to my knee.' Sheila jumped out of the water like a cricket. We raced about, picking up our washing where we had them spread out on the stone and bush by the side of the river. 'Come come, make haste. Make haste; let's get out of the river. Let's cross on the other side.'

We dashed about, picked up the clothes as quickly as possible. Some wet, some still dirty. The water was almost covering the flat stone we used to jump on to cross the river. Leaves and bits of rubbish floated down. The water became like when you dig potato and wash out the mud.

As we reached the bank I looked back to see if we left anything behind. 'O Gawd,' I gasped. 'Lawd Sheila, look. Look, Miss Sagoo down there. She don't hear the river coming.'

'Bunjay!' She gasped, and started to shout to the woman. 'Miss Sagoo, Miss Sagoo,' she shouted. 'The river coming. Miss Sagoo make haste, the river coming down.' The woman carried on cho-chooing the pair of old dungarees. The only thing that mattered in the world was she and the dungarees. Me and Sheila shouted and shouted. All the time we could hear the river rumbling, tumbling down the mountain.

'Run down there and call her, Flora,' Sheila shouted. 'Run, quick. The river coming fast.'

'Miss Sagoo, Miss Sagoo! The river coming down. Quick, pick up your clothes,' I shouted, as I raced to where she was. Waving my hands about like a mad person. 'Miss Sagoo, the river, the river coming down. Please hear me.' I was shouting and pleading with her in my head to hear me. At last she lifted her head, as if coming out of a dream.

'Quick,' I said. 'The river coming down. Cross on the other side.'

'What you say gal? Who coming?'

'The river! It coming down. Look how the water dirty!'

'What you mean river coming down? Whey de rain for river to come down?'

'I think it fall in the mountain. Hurray up,' I shouted. Doop, doop a doop ruck a tuck tuck, the water was tumbling nearer and nearer. I was getting panicky, because what I was saying did not really soak in the woman head.

'Aye aye,' she registered at last. 'Aaye but look how the water dirty nuh! The river look coming down for true. I better hurry up.'

'Make haste and cross over,' I prodded. 'Hurry.' At last, at last, she noticed the water. I felt relieved. She dashed about as if she had spring in the body. In one last swoop she bundled the washing in the basin and dashed on the bank to safety. I went back to meet Sheila. We put our basins on our heads and started dwaddling home. Just as we reached the damson tree, I don't know what made Sheila look back, but I heard her bellow: 'Oh no!'

I turned around to see Miss Sagoo's basin on the ground and she in the middle of the river heading for the other side. The heavy water was only a few yards away.

'Miss Sagoo, don't go,' we both shouted. 'Come back, come back.' We tried to shout above the noise of the rumbling water.

'I going for me petticoat,' the woman screeched. 'I forget me petti . . . ' She did not finished what she was saying. The water rushed on her like a tidal wave. She raised her hands

9

in front her as if trying to hold back the water. One woosh shoosh goosh – right in front our eyes she was swallowed inside the bowel of the water. Swallowed up . . . gone . . . gone . . .

Sheila and I screamed and bawled and screamed and bawled. Crowds of people were quickly by the river. Some were on the bridge, few yards further up. They saw the whole thing. Men began running down the bay road towards the sea, peeping and searching as they went. Others used long bamboo to poke into the water as far out as they could reach. Everybody searched and searched. Some women were crying. Children running between everybody trying to see what was happening. After the first few minutes, me and Sheila were dumbed. I felt dead inside. I closed my eyes to stop seeing Miss Sagoo's face as the water swallowed her. The only thing they found after all the searching was a nice white frilly petticoat hanging on a black sage bush.

Three days later Mr Joe going to raise his fishpot early in the morning, down in the stone hole between Marigot and Blackbay, noticed a piece of cloth tangled up between the stone. He said he thought it strange because he was sure that it was not there when he set the fish pot the night before. Anyway he rowed his little boat nearer and had a little poke inside the hole with his oar. He said at first his body felt sort of funny. He could not say exactly how, but he knew something was not right. He said he used one of his hook and sort of pull out the piece of cloth, was then he noticed something like a person foot. Well he never rowed a boat so hard in all the years he fishing. He pulled up in Marigot bay and bawled out that a body was stuffed in the stone hole. Was like the whole place catch a fire – Concorde, Marigot Grand Roy, the whole place. To begin with they started

10

saying is somebody who killed somebody or the other and stuff the body down there. Quick quick they started saying is Jaspar that kill somebody to pay off the devil. At first nobody thought about it being Miss Sagoo because was miles from where the river took her away, so nobody would think that she would be dragged so far, all the way from Grand Roy.

That was one of the strangest thing that happened in Grenada. Years later people still talked about how the river take the woman high dry season. Imagine, Lent season – everything parched dry, sun splitting earth, farmer want to burn their lands but 'fraid to light fire in case it get away and no water to put it out. No rain for weeks and just like that river come down . . . even after that still no rain. Everybody said it was a sign . . . Papa God coming. Church people started preaching louder that people must repent . . . make peace with God. Everyday a different preacher turn up in the foreroad. Some Sundays there are about three or four different groups preaching. Miss Sagoo's daughter came from Trinidad. People didn't even know if that woman alive or dead. Me I didn't know Miss Sagoo had any children. Apparently the woman left Grenada and went overseas years ago, first to Venezuela, then they say she lived somewhere in the Virgin Islands before she settled down in Trinidad. She only came back to Grenada once to see her mother, then she went back, saying Grenada too slow for her. The woman face looked like an old horse and she stupid like some old donkey.

Me and Sheila suffered from shock since the death. Sometimes in the night in bed I hear the river and when I tried to close my eyes is Miss Sagoo I seeing. That was bad enough, but when that woman came and saying is we caused the river to take her mother, well I tell you I almost turn a mental case. She said we should of seen the petticoat hanging on the bush and go and get it instead of letting her old mother try to cross the river again. She went on about how we waited until the river was near before we called out, knowing that the old woman was deaf as bat.

With that woman coming from Trinidad and running her mouth and other people saying how they see the dead woman standing on the river stone, I became very sick. All I did was think about what happened. Always having headaches.

To make matters worse, about three months after all the ruction a woman came from Happy Hill telling Mammy about how she had a dream about me, and Mammy must let her bathe me. Apparently she had to boil all kind of bush, take me to the busherie foreday morning before first cock crow and bathe me. She said that she had special power to drive out evil spirit. She said if Mammy didn't do what she says something bad would happen to me. Mammy run behind the woman. Told her not to bring her damn stupidness in front her door, if anybody had evil spirit on them, was her . . . If is she nastiness she to want to practice, she better go and find somebody else. Then the school children started teasing me and Sheila saying we have lajabless on us. It affected me worse than Sheila, still when her mother said she'll send her to Tivoli to her cousin for a while she was glad to go, because she didn't like school anyway. Me, it was different because I liked school, so even when Sheila said I should ask Mammy to let me go with her, I said no. I didn't want when I come back for the girls in the class to laugh at me because I did not know the subject. I knew they didn't like me already because they say I was too small to be in the same class with them. Some of them have 15 and 16

12

and still in standard four, so was shame they shame because I only had 12.

Some of them, especially Shirley and Norma, used to make see a lot of trouble. When all these things with Miss Sagoo happened they even used to beat me up. For months afterwards I was not happy at all, not at school, not at home. Mammy was really worried that something would happen to me – especially when people started saying how Miss Sagoo haunting the place. Miss Mae, who lived behind Miss Moore, by where she used to keep the school, said she saw something. Miss Moore had the little private school there for a few years. She used to take in children under 5. That was a very good thing because some mothers didn't have time to look after the little children, so for at least during the morning they would go to school where they would learn to write the A B C and get something to eat breakfast time.

The lady running the school good good. As soon as her husband come from America he made her close it down saying he don't want her mixing with all those common people. I don't know who he think he is, because he come from a big country he want to show off on people, thinking he better than even the people he used to go to school with. The trouble was although he didn't want his wife to even talk with the people in the village, it didn't take him long to start running after all the young girls. Joanna, Sheila's sister, the girl was working in a Syrian store in town good good, helping out her mother with the house and thing, after a while I noticed I didn't see her; when I asked Sheila for her she said I too damn farse, I must mind my own business. I was surprised. I didn't find that was farsness at all; I don't go about minding people business, and I told her that. A little while afterwards she told that her sister making baby for Mr Moore and they send her to stay with a godmother in Grenville. Not only the young girls he used to interfere with; that big woman with all those children behind the post office. I don't know what was going on between them, but the woman used to go in the market on Saturdays with Miss Mae – all of a sudden, as if she turn big shot, she don't even want to talk to anybody. Not just that, when Miss Moore used to run the little school, she used to help out Miss Margaret, sometimes giving her two days' work to help her out with the children, even taking the smaller ones on the school without money because the mother could not afford it. Then what happen, eh? What happen, next thing people started talking how is at Miss Margaret Mr Moore does sleep. The woman don't have any shame, she even go to the man house and curse his wife. I never see that before.

Anyway, as I was saying before about Miss Mae seeing something! Was early on Saturday morning she getting ready to pick up Lago Pride for the first trip to town. Everybody trying to go down early to catch the sale, especially as the tourist boat came in the Friday night. That morning Miss Mae sent Anson ahead with a basket of provision. She was only two minutes behind him. She said, as she reached a few yards before where Miss Sagoo had put down the basin to go back for her petticoat, she saw this white thing in the road. At first she thought was Mr Boyce goat that broke the rope. Then as she got nearer her head started sort of swelling up and perspiration started pouring down her back as if she had a bucket of water leaking on her head. She said she felt as if somebody was walking beside her. She had her eyes fixed on the thing in the road. Somehow she knew it was no goat. She got so frightened she could not move. She did not even blink her eyes, yet the thing disappeared . . . just like that. One second it was there, the next it vanished . . . gone. Then when she sort of glanced out of the corner of her eyes to the river, she saw the shadow of a woman flash in the water. Miss Mae said she had to say five 'Hail Mary' and three 'Our Father' before she could move. Was a good thing Anson did not see it. He sure would of mess himself.

When she reached by the road and told the people what she had seen, they said she is not the first person to see the dead woman. They said because of the way she died her soul was restless, she needed prayers to help her to rest in peace. One of the women said that one day she was washing on the big stone on the side of where the accident happened. She said she was alone in the river, but she heard a cho koo choo chook chook as if somebody scrubbing clothes. When she lifted her head she saw Miss Sagoo plain plain as when she was alive – same red check dress with the old straw hat on her head. It took her a few seconds to remember the woman was dead . . . by then she had disappeared. People started to be frightened to go to the river so they decided to make a prayer for the dead. After that things settled down.

It must be about four years since all that happened, but seeing Miss O'Brien standing in the sea stone making maca-quee reminded me of all these things. I wanted to run back but I need the slipper fixed. I couldn't go all the way to Concorde with piece of slipper on my foot and I couldn't go back to change it because was the only one I had to knock about in. I had my good church shoes and a crêpe sole to go to school, that was all. Mammy said if my uncle in England send us some money for Christmas she would buy me a new one for church, then I could go to school with the church shoes and knock about with the crêpe sole. Was Tanty Floris

15

that gave me the slipper when she came from Trinidad. She brought other things for us. I thought that was very nice of her. Mammy worked very hard to look after me and my brother. She tried her best but sometimes we had to do without, because it's she alone and she didn't work for a lot of money.

Since I had about 2 and my brother Christopher 3½ my father went to St. Croix. Mammy said at the time he said he only gone for three years to raise a few dollars to come back and look after his family. The first year he wrote every month. He always used to cry trouble, saying how things hard and he can't find work. He used to say how the little money he had he had to spend on rent and food which was very expensive. Mammy said she didn't mind if he couldn't send anything for us as long as he looked after himself. Then when he wrote and said he got job she was looking for things to be better. Only once or twice he put ten dollars in a letter for us. After that not a line from him. All write; she write him; nothing. Years and years past we heard nothing from him. Then one day Miss Melda sister came back home. She travelled all over the place. Once I heard Miss Melda saying the sister left Venezuela and went to the Virgin Islands. Now, apparently, she settle down in St. Croix. Anyway I heard her telling Mammy that she saw my father in St. Croix and how he working for good money, but spending all in rum shop and not looking after himself. Miss Irma said the man changed. He was such a nice man when she first meet him in St. Croix, just as he was when he was home. Always on about his nice family in Grenada. How he saving his money to go to them, then bit by bit as if they wash hand on him. He just let himself go.

'Chupes,' Mammy sucked her teeth. 'Wash hand on him!

Worthless he worthless. Who could wash hand on you to make you forget you family . . . your own flesh and blood.'

That same evening, Mammy sent me to the post office to buy an airmail envelope and two writing paper for her. After dinner she started tumbling in a drawer with some old letters. When I asked her what she was looking for she said an address. The way she said it I know she didn't want to tell me about it. I thought it was to do with somebody in England. I couldn't think who it was because if it was my uncle she would of said. The only other person I could think of was Boca cousin Melda boy, but then I don't understand why she would write him. When Boca left Grenada he said he going to Africa to find his family; the next thing we heard cousin Melda saying the man in England, saying he meet an African cousin and trying to work to find some money to go to Africa with him. Mammy said that side of the family lie too much. I don't really know how they come to be our family. One day I asked my grandmother how they come to be our family. When you look at it there is no resemblance at all. She said her mother and cousin Melda grandmother used to live next door in Shantimel. The two old women father grew up together in St. Vincent and they came to Grenada the same time as young men. Since that time they say they are family. People really strange; I don't see how that could make them family.

Coming back to Boca and him going to Africa. I don't know where he think Africa is, or come to think of it how he would find anybody when he don't even know where to start. I think cousin Melda say about that African man he met in England to take out shame in her eye. They must be think Africa is like going to Trinidad; they don't realise the place is a big big continent. Even though our great great

17

great grandparents were brought to the West Indies as slaves from Africa, I think he should of done some research to find out what part of Africa his people came from, if they came from Africa at all. I don't know how he would of found out all these things when they were not teaching about these in school. Was as if these people did not exist before they brought them to the West Indies. As if we had no past. Those boys used to tease Boca, saying he too ugly; nobody in Africa would own him. He told them they are the stupid ones, all they fit for was sitting down by the roadside talking stupidness instead of reading books. The more he called them stupid the more they laughed at him. I think that's why he made up his mind definitely to go. He did say that he got a message in a sleep, that he must go to Africa. These people always blaming their lies on dreams.

The night before he left, cousin Melda made a big prayer meeting for him. It was just like a wake, with rice porridge and saltfish souse and bread all night, and don't talk about the white rum. It was really like a wake without a dead body. People came from Grenville and danced African dance all night. Next morning Boca well dress up went around the village saying goodbye to everybody. That was the last time we heard of Boca for a long time. It was good that he was travelling but a bit sad as well, especially as he was cousin Melda one boy and he always so helpful and willing.

2

Six months after cousin Melda made the prayer for Boca, Miss Adina decided she must make one too. I tell you Grenada people is something. We know Miss O'Brien was crazy, but to tell the truth between she and Miss Adina I don't know who was worst. The older they got they crazier they became. Not losing their mind with age or anything like that, nuh . . . nothing was wrong with their minds, they have more rememberings than any young person. They were both old but Miss O'Brien was much older, she must have well over one hundred. Well, about Miss Adina and her prayer meeting. The woman lived near to us, in fact we had to pass under her window along the little track to get to our house. The track run sort of between her house and Mr Nobel. The evening of the prayers when I came from school she was in front her door. She had a long table all laid out with nice white table cloth and shinny wares and things, right under the immortelle tree. She was busy busy taking up the red immortelle flowers between the glasses and things. The truth is I didn't want her to see me because I know what Mammy already said, so I was trying to pass quiet quiet for her not to see me. I forgot that the piece of galvanise across

19

the drain was shaking, as I stepped on it plopp, flopp, I ended in the drain.

'Flora you comin tonite?' she said, lifting her head. 'Tell Joyce she mus sen you . . . you hear.'

'Yes Miss Adina,' I answered. 'I go tell her as soon as she come.'

'I know Joyce is a funny woman, but I hope she let you come. Everybody coming, big people as well, not only children so she could come too.'

'Yes Miss Adina,' I said again. I really wanted to go to the prayer meeting, but Mammy already said she not letting me follow that crazy woman in her stupidness. Everybody knew how Miss Adina was, so when she mentioned about the prayers we said perhaps it's a good thing. Maybe a little prayers would help her change. When she is not at home Cacoben Hill is a different place, nice and quiet. I mean people make still noise and even curse each other, but it was different to what Miss Adina carried on with. When she is around all you hear is cursing and quarrelling day and night . . . just cursing and quarrelling. Sometimes late late in the night we can't sleep in peace. And the things she said!' Once she told everybody that a man keep following her everywhere she went. Nobody ever seen that man.

Another night about 2 o'clock she bellowed out one 'O Gawd papa bunjay oye' that everybody had to rush out of their beds to find out what was wrong. Mammy called. Mr Nobel called. No answer, only a forever 'Doup doup, bang a lang pang, o gawd papa bunja look at me trouble,' coming from her house.

Mr Nobel left his house in the darkness and go over to see what was wrong. By the time he reached in front her door she was half way down the road bawling. Before first cock crow she was back quarrelling. We were very worried, wondering if was really something wrong with her this time. Thinking perhaps somebody interfered with her. As soon as she reached her yard, Mammy called and asked what was wrong.

'Saye saye oye,' she said. 'Saye saye I never see dat in my life. Not in all my life and look how much grey hair in my head.'

I was still in my bed but I wasn't asleep. Nobody could sleep anyway.

'Last night I lie down in my bed,' she went on. 'On my bed you know, quiet inside my room. I lie down in my bed with my bible under my pillow and dat priest come inside my house and put sweets in my mouth telling me to suck.'

'Priest! In you house . . . in the night?!' Mammy sounded baffled.

'Yeh saye saye. I know who it was. Is that new priest they have in Grenville. Yesterday I see him in town. We talk good good. He look at me in the poke of my eyes all the time is work he working on me.'

'Chupes,' Mammy said, and went into the kitchen.

After that she started coming up with all sort of things. Sometimes she would burn all kind of things around the house, making the whole smell like doctor shop. When she first talked about the prayer meeting she said it was because she heard they were fighting war in England and the prayers is to prevent her one child from being killed. I don't know what fighting in England had to do with her daughter who was in Tobago. Two weeks before the date she said she would be keeping the prayers, on the Monday she went up to Gouyave. She said for a few days. Peace at last, even for a few days. One day I asked Mammy which church she

21

having the prayers, Mammy said she didn't know, because since the woman said priest put sweets in her mouth she stopped going to church.

The following Sunday she came home. I don't know how to describe it, but she was different. I don't mean different in size or colour, nothing like that. She was the same tall wiry dry-up woman. Deep bronzy face, long and sharpen like little cutlass. Eyes squint up yippy yippe like fireflies, but there was a sort of calmness about her. Because I felt she was different I felt a bit frightened of her. When she came I was sweeping the drain below the kitchen window. She called to tell me she was home. I looked at the woman; she stared straight in my eyes. I tell you I felt funny. I felt as jumbie was playing with me. Afterwards I told Mammy about it; she said I should be careful with the woman.

Monday evening she came in our yard. 'Joyce oye,' she called. 'Look nuh, take that few grain a jacks.' She had a calabash of jacks which she handed to Mammy. 'Doh forget the prayer meeting, you know Joyce,' she said. 'Doh forget I having it on Thursday. You must send Flora and you must come too.'

'Alright,' Mammy said. 'I remember. We go come.'

Tuesday night she called again to remind us. 'Which church you having it in?' Mammy asked.

'Church; who tell you I going in any church?' The woman almost bit off Mammy head. 'I not going in no church.' Mammy opened her mouth and eyes at the same time, as if she seeing jumbie. I was sitting on the step by the pan of jump-up-and-kiss-me. I looked up at Mammy, and then at Miss Adina where she was standing in front the kitchen. She two hands on her waist as if she ready to make confusion.

'I doh know who tell you people I going in any church,'

she started. 'I starting the procession in the gap under the window. We passing down by cousin Tin boli tree to go to the busherie.'

'Aye,' Mammy said. 'I didn't know is salacca you making Miss Adina.'

'Salacca! Who tell you anything about salacca?' Miss Adina snapped. 'You this Joyce stupid too much. I tell you I having a little prayer for me daughter, you come talking about salacca. Is Mr Marcelle coming to make it? He don't know anything about salacca. Is those African people in Grenville that does make that kind of prayers. They say them is African but they lie too much. I know one of them good good. The time they come in Palmiste she come all dress up like them African thinking nobody know her. But she is Miss Ully granddaughter. Her mother belongs right here. Is when that man, I don't remember his name, but he came from overseas with his mouth full of gold teeth. Is when he came here she followed him down the bottom side. So I don't know how she come saying she is African.'

Mammy didn't say anything, just pammed her lips tight and rolled her eyes.

As I was saying, the evening of the prayer meeting when I came from school, Miss Adina was picking off flowers from the table she had dressed up with all new glasses, knives plates and things, under the immortelle tree. Before I reached level with her front yard I smelled the food. When I looked in the yard there were three strange women moving about. There were also two more tables in the yard. One in front the kitchen, and the other under the damson tree on the other side of the house. On the tables there were plates of all kinds of food – fried fresh fish, fried saltfish, saltfish souse, bakes, rock cakes, coconut turnover all kinds of things. My belly

23

started to rumble, my mouth dripping water, just smelling the food. Apart from the food there were bunches of flowers spread out on the ground as when people bring wreaths for funeral.

About five o'clock people started gathering by the road. They stand up all down by Miss Thelma little parlour. A little while after Mr Marcelle and his people arrived. Since the bus break round Boawden Corner you hear the noise. 'Boaw boaw boaw', they pound the side of the bus, while bashing the tambourine and shaking the bolie seed, shak shak. And the singing, Lord you should of heard them. Mind you it was more shouting than singing. I don't understand how Miss Adina say is not African prayer. Mr Marcelle and his people were dressed same like the Grenville people and some of the things they did were the same. The only difference was they did not go to the busherie and they killed animals for food. Sometimes I wish I could find a book to learn about these things. To understand the differences; like why Miss Adina meeting is different from cousin Melda.

Well about cousin Melda and Boca; that is something else. Boca left saying he going to Africa. All of a sudden cousin Melda come up with story that he had to go to England to make up papers before he could get to Africa. Every time you ask her for her son she come up with a different story. The last one was Boca meet up a man from Mozambique who said that he knows Boca family in Africa and he will take Boca back with him to meet them. These family in Mozambique supposed to be on his father side. Mammy said she never know people could lie so. She said she don't know how Boca could meet up his father family when as far as she knows the boy never know his father. She said cousin Melda never told anybody who was Boca father. Now out of the

24

blues the son going to Africa to settle down and then send for his mother. I never hear this in all my life. I don't know how cousin Melda come with this story at all. Well shame really came home to her when teacher Mark come home from England where he was studying. He said he saw Boca in England and the young man was a disgrace. Wouldn't find work to do. Spending all his time gambling and drinking. I think that was too much for cousin Melda; the next thing we knew was she packed her bag and went to Aruba. To be truthful I couldn't believe what teacher Mark said about Boca. I mean he was such a nice, decent young man.

I don't know; when people travel as if something take over their soul. Look at my father. Everybody say how he was a nice nice man when he was home. Now he in that place he don't have time for us. As if they wash his brain with bad water or something. Although Mammy say is worthless he worthless, I know she does think about him. She think about him more especially when she hear the state he was in. Would you believe it; years we don't hear anything, then all of a sudden we start hearing all kinds of things. Mammy don't seem surprise, though. You would think she expecting the news. It was like when I told her what happened to teacher Marion's wedding. She wasn't surprised at all. Anyway, years we don't hear anything about my father, then all of a sudden we hearing all kind of news. The same week Mammy got a letter from Aunty Floris in Trinidad. She said she met up with a woman who used to live over the river in Grand Roy. That woman is actually living in St. Croix but gone to Trinidad for holiday. They started beating mouth just like old times, one thing lead to another, and then the woman mentioned my father and the state he is in St. Croix. I could imagine them beating mouth, just like when Mammy and

Miss Chrissie sit down on the step beating mouth. They go on and on for ages. You should hear the big laugh they used to let go. Sometimes I well want to hear what they saying, but I know Mammy would cut my skin if she see me listening to big people talk. Aunty Floris said she felt so bad when she heard how this nice nice man stay in other people country and turn bazoodie that she had to send to tell Mammy.

Mammy is a funny woman; very funny. One minute she quarrelling saying is how he make bed so he go lie down, and if you plant pease you can't reap corn and things like that; the next she would sit with her hand under her chin looking sad sad. At first when I asked her what's wrong she said nothing, she only thinking how to make life. But I know her too much. I know when she is worried about things, especially when she started talking to herself and chupsing chupsing. When I asked her again what's wrong she said how she feel sorry for my father. She said she know he never bother with us when he was on his foot, but after all he is still my father. She even say she was thinking if she went to St. Croix he might come back home with her. I just looked at her.

Three weeks after that Aunty Floris came home on holiday. She is not really my aunty. I mean not my mother or father sister. She and Mammy grew up together; apparently they did everything together that people used to say they more than blood sisters. I love her very much, more than my real aunt. For a start I don't like Aunty Bella at all. She is my father sister. She living in America now. Mammy said one time the woman came back on holiday you would think she was Miss America or something. She cock up her bam, skin up her mouth as if she see mess. She always used to play white, even when she was at school, especially as she was a little light skin. Well, since she in America it was worse. Mammy said the woman so stupid. She came with a big red wig on her head. And her skin patchy patchy yellow. I hear is cream they use to bleach their skin. I call that real stupid. I don't see anything wrong with my nice smooth black skin. I remember when Aunty Bella came. I had about 5, I think. I saw this woman standing on the step in the police station, and Miss Chrissie told me is my aunty. I must say howdy. The woman look at me as if I was dirty. I ran home crying. Mammy was really vex. From that I don't even like to hear the woman name call. As far as I concern, Aunty Floris is my real aunt. When she came on holiday she brought a parcel with all kinds of things for us. She had the slipper wrapped up by itself. She had worn it a little but I didn't mind.

I used to wear it to catechism class in Gouyave on Saturday mornings. Before all that botheration with Miss Sagoo, me and Sheila used to walk up Gouyave road together good good, then when she came back from Tivoli she said she going back to Catholic church. I don't understand that family at all. Some go to Catholic church sometimes, then one might go to the Anglican. Then after a while all of them would go to one church or not at all. Sheila used to go to the Catholic church every Sunday, then when I told her I started taking lessons to take my first communion and then prepare for confirmation she said she coming to the Anglican church with me. I told her she can't do that. She got vex. She said I don't know anything. All church is church and she could go to any one she like to take the sacraments. She said her mother said it doesn't matter where you worship as long as you have a clean heart.

I don't know where all that about having clean heart comes

in because some of these people that go to church every Sunday, big big bible under their arm, are nothing but devils. Some of them well dress up but look in their faces and is the devil you see written straight across. If you pass under the church window during the service, the way they shouting when they singing you would think they having competition to see who God would hear first. Sometimes if you watch them for a few minutes you see how they eyeing up each other clothes. No wonder Mammy says she not sending me there at all, even if it is nearer home. She said some of these people who pretend to be the pillars in the church so wicked she don't know how God don't strike them down. Then she would always add 'God is a merciful God in truth'. Still that's where Sheila used to go until she wanted to follow me, just to make first communion. When I told her she would have to ask the priest she got more vex.

'Show off you want to show,' she shouted at me.

'Aaye; what you mean show off? What I show off about?!'

'Must show off you want to show yes. Me and you going to government school, but you don't want me to come in in Gouyave with you to church.'

'Girl you stupid yes. If you want to go to Gouyave what I have to do with that, eh?! Is not me business. You going on as if Gouyave is mines.'

'You know what I mean. Don't play you don't know.' She looked at my slipper, then at the black crêpe sole she was wearing.

'Chupes.' I shook my head. 'Nothing wrong with you crêpe, you know. If you want to come in Anglican church, I not stopping you.'

She came to the church with me for a little while. Even starting taking catechism lessons to make first communion.

28

Then all these things with Miss Sagoo happened. When Sheila came back from Tivoli she went back to her old church, saying it is nearer to home. I know she was lying because she never complained about the journey before.

I hear all kinds of stories about what used to happen in the church, especially when they having choir practice. Different gossip since that new priest took over. Is not everything you hear is true. When hot sun bursting people head they make up all kind of lies, so sometimes you hear things and keep your mouth shut. But other times you begin to think to yourself that it must be true, especially when you hear it from people you know don't usually listen to gossip. People like Miss Chrissie. I heard her talking to Mammy one morning. She was vex vex, although like Mammy Miss Chrissie never really get vex. So whatever she was telling Mammy must be true and upset her very much. Mammy always say I too damn farse. She said I mustn't listen when I hear big people talking. She strange though, because although she don't want me to listen to big conversation, still when she see Miss Edna and Mr Jones talking in the gap she asking me what they talking about. The same way sometimes she beating me. Plaw plaw, plat a plaw she pounding my skin with licks. The same time she shouting at me to shut up. Plap, stip, plataw, licks burning my skin as when you pour salt on sore foot, yet I must shut up. Sometimes when she beating me, she would say things like if I don't shut up she would give me something to cry for. And the trouble was sometimes I don't even know what she beating me for, because I sure didn't do anything. That morning she and Miss Chrissie was talking. Miss Chrissie was standing under the soursop tree. I don't know how she like under that tree so. The tree is nothing but black ants, and so the soursop sour when it ripe. You can only use it make babalay. When Miss Chrissie is not sitting on the step beating mouth with Mammy she would be standing under that tree. Anyway Mammy was leaning over the kitchen window talking to the woman. I didn't hear what they were saying at first. I was busy cleaning out the flower garden. Then Mammy said, sort of sharp sharp, 'You sure Miss Chrissie, you sure?!' When I heard that my head sort of jerk up.

'Aaye; how you mean if I sure? You think I go tell you if is not true?' Miss Chrissie say. She then moved from under the tree and went and sat on the step in front the kitchen. Mammy went in front the kitchen. I still cleaning the flowers.

'Well,' Miss Chrissie started again. 'You know Jane. She don't meddle with people. I was frightened when she burst in the house last night. I thought somebody was after her to kill her or something.'

The only sound that Mammy made was a sort of 'aaaaye'.

When I heard Jane's name call I knew something bad had happened. Earlier I was waiting outside Miss Thelma parlour for the bread van when I noticed Mollie and Christophine talking secret secret. Then Christophine shouted 'Bonjay oye look at we trouble nuh; de man come play God. Pretending to help people . . . now look at trouble nuh.' When she remember I was standing close to them, she cut eyes at me and shut her mouth, so I move and went and stand on the step in front the police station. Was then I saw Miss Chrissie husband inside the station. Not in front the door or even on the verandah where people usually stand up, but right inside. The way he was waving his hands about and shouting, you could see he was well vex. Now Miss Chrissie talking to Mammy, calling Jane name and she look well vex, I sort of move a little nearer the kitchen and listen. She said something but I couldn't hear, was sort of 'shsh . . . shuss . . . shuing.'

Jane was Miss Chrissie second daughter. She had about sixteen years, but she wasn't afraid of anything. She was a very nice girl as well. Very polite and helpful. Everybody liked her, especially the older people. First thing they would say to us when they catch us misbehaving is 'You nutting like Jane. Why you doh behave like Jane?'

'Aye aye Miss Joyce,' Miss Chrissie braced her back against the side of the kitchen. Put her two hands on her waist as if supporting her back brace. 'Priest you know, Miss Joyce. God priest.'

'Lawd! What she father say?' Mammy asked. 'Eh, what he say? She tell him aready?!'

I thought of how I saw Mr Campbell in the station earlier on mad mad, like he ready to fight.

'She didn't have to tell him. He was in the house when she come crying. Lawd; Miss Joyce I had to hold the man. He pick up his cutlass, ready to go up to the rectory. Aaye.'

'Woye oyoye,' Mammy plapped her hands. 'Wooye! I could imagine. Mr Campbell is a quiet man, just like his daughter. They don't trouble people, but to see his child in that state . . . boy oh boy I could just imagine.' They were quiet for a few minutes, then Mammy asked sort of quiet like, 'Miss Chrissie; he didn't . . . I mean Father Jacob; he didn't touch Jane, nuh? He didn't bring his farseness in front her, nuh?'

'He,' Miss Chrissie closed her eyes. Covered her mouth with one hand. 'Priest you know! God priest.' She was quiet again. Mammy put her hand around the other woman shoulder, consoling her. At the same giving me a little cut eye.

'What kind a man is that, eh?!' Miss Chrissie starting talking again. 'Jane said he took them to the vestry saying as it's a few of them, they could practise there. First thing he did was take off his collar and surplice. She said she sat waitin to see what would happen. She already heard gossip, so she was waiting.'

'You mean Jane went there to catch him?' Mammy asked. 'She really brave.'

'Something so. You know Jane. If she see things wrong she go open her mouth. You know all that talk that going on about what the priest up to. Well it look as if Jane wanted to find out for herself, that is why she and her friend went to choir practice last night. Well she said when they go in the vestry, the priest take out his clothes, and she noticed how two of the girls move close close to him. Sort of rubbing themselves on him. Then bold as brass Miss Etta girl hug the man and kiss he plam on his mouth.'

'What!' Mammy hailed out. 'You mean she kiss the priest so?'

'Saye, saye, right in front of them. No shame, nothing. He pushed her away and said not tonight. Jane said the girl plump down on a chair and starting giving her bad eye. She was shocked. Then to make bad worse, without a word the priest took Jane hymn book from her, threw it on the table, pulled her to him and pushed his mouth in hers, the same time trying to kneed her breast.'

'Papa Bunjay oye have mercy, have mercy.' This time Mammy really hailed out. 'Bunjay, Miss Chrissie, what this world comin to, eh? What God world coming to? No wonder Mr Campbell was going up there with his cutlass.'

Miss Chrissie shook her head, up down, left right, up down. Her eyes close real tight. I got frightened thinking something might happen to her. You know she might drop down right in front our door. I remember when we went to a forty-days prayer meeting Mr Alec had for his grandson they killed in England, the woman from Marigot went very funny. Everybody was singing hymns and things, then all of a sudden the woman just sat down in the middle of the room shaking. The same way she was shaking her head with her eyes close. Then she started talking all sort of stupidness, even tried to take out Mr Alec trousers, saying she in the 'spirit'. Mammy said it was all old tricks. Some of these people had curse on them. I don't know how Mammy knows all these things. I know Miss Chrissie is nothing like that, but seeing how she on the step frightened me a little. I looked at Mammy. She looked at me.

'He asked for trouble,' Miss Chrissie went, quieter than before. 'As he put his mouth on hers, she pushed him away and slapp plapp her hand landed across his face. She said she was so vex she didn't have time to think whether he was priest or no priest. As he did that she just box him down.'

'Woye! he asked for it. I sure Papa God wouldn't punish her. Is He give her the strength to stand up to that man who say he is priest,' Mammy reassured her friend.

As I listened to them talking I began to think of why Sheila so hot to go back to that church. She on and on about Father Jacob. Everything Father Jacob this, Father Jacob that. How he working to make the choir the best in the island that they can go and sing on the radio on Sunday evenings. Hem; better, my foot.

This Father Jacob came to the parish for good when old Father Gibbs retired. Everybody loved the old priest. He spent almost all his life in the village. He was one of us. No matter what religion you were, if you sick or in trouble he

33

was there. When he retired everybody who went to his fare-well fête in the big Roman Catholic school cried. We all knew we were going to miss him very much. Although he had his own school and church to look after, yet he helped everybody else. Like when hurricane Janet blew off the Government school roof. The Government said they could only afford to patch up what's left. Father Gibbs wrote letters to colleagues in England and Ireland and raised enough money to put a new roof on the school and do other repairs to his own school building. Jane worked closely with Father Gibbs. He used to encourage the people in whatever they want to do to help themselves and others. When he left it was like a piece of the village was taken away. The thing is, when you getting on in years you have to take things easy. About five years before he left for good he was very sick. He went to England for a big operation, then spent a couple of months in his own country. Even while he should be resting to get better, he was still raising money to help Gren-ada. When he came back he had raised enough for a brand new piano for the school, and brought someone over with him to repair the church organ. When he came back he talked more and more about Ireland. People said his spirit wants to rest in his native land. The spirits were calling him back across the waters. About eighteen months after he came back he became sick again, this time at 80 he decide to retire and return home. We were surprised when he said he had 80 years. He looked like somebody who had about 60.

For months after he went back to Ireland the church was without a proper priest. Mr Bolam and sometimes Mr Peters used to take prayers. Then a priest came from St. Lucia for a little while. He only stayed about six months. They said he was not a full priest. He had to go to Italy to finish his

34

training. I thought that was funny. I mean I never thought people had to train to be priest the way you train to be a doctor or somebody like that. I thought God told you to preach and you did it like Boysie. Everyday he in the rum shop drinking the old Lasagesse. As soon as he get pay instead of giving his poor mother something, he would sit under the balcony in the rum shop with the other rum men, drinking rum. Every time you see Boysie he drunk drunk; next thing is one morning Boysie dancing about in the foreroad with bible in his hand saying he got the message from God. Everybody thought he was drunk. All true church people were vex vex, saying he using God's book and God's name in vain. Papa God will punish him. For a whole week Boysie in the foreroad with his bible preaching, telling everbody he had the message from God. He went into the same rum shop he used to drink, telling the same people he used to drink with to turn away from their evil ways, repent and give their hearts to God.

One day I was down the road, me and Sheila getting water when we heard one ruction going on in Mr Mace shop, shouting, cussing all bad word – then a doop, bloob, plump, blaap in the road. Every body run by the police station and the shop to see what was happening. There was a young police from St. Davids in the station at the time. He came out and just lean over the balcony watching. Although we all heard the doop, bloob, plaap and cussing, no one actually bawled out 'murder, police'. When we had a good look, is Boysie we see on the ground grabbling in the dust for his bible and the specs he started wearing. It wasn't a proper specs either. His mother used to wear them years ago when she first came from Trinidad. I don't know what was worse shame for Boysie, the way he was kicked out of the shop

35

and everybody holding their belly laughing, or his mother coming shouting at him how he is a damn pappyshow in the place. I don't know what he expected. He know what they like. One minute you a rum sucker, then you trying to tell people you turn preacher. And the thing is, he went in the same rum shop preaching. Mr Mace told him to get out. The other men told him to get out, he is a devil and a damn liar. He should stop taking God's name in vain. Instead of the man leaving the shop, he kneel down by the counter close to the rum bar, take a candle from his pocket, light it, then opened his bible. At first everybody in the shop just watched him. They couldn't believe their eyes. When Mr Mace realised what was really happening. Watch good good what Boysie was doing. He jumped over the counter, picked up Boysie by the breeches and pelt him outside like a bag of manure. Then pelt his bible after him. With that all hell let loose. The men started shouting and cussing Boysie. It was not only Boysie they were cussing . . . just cussing bad word. After that Boysie disappeared. Next thing we heard he in St. David building church.

There are others that started preaching that way . . . getting message in dream. Not go and train like that St. Lucia priest. As I said there were others. For instance, Miss Marina daughter, the one they use to tease 'picky hair'. The woman went to Trinidad to meet she child father, two years later she come back with two children saying she had the 'call'. The story came back to Grenada that she had to run from the place because the authority was after her. I never found out why. Mammy says when these people conscience beating, after thiefing and wickedness they saying they turn to God. But God turn back on some of them.

Then there's this other woman. I felt really sorry for her.

She was living by the big school gap. Hers was the first house you meet before turning up the hill. Miss Joycelyn was a nice lady in government work and everything. She used to help out in the school as well, when we having fête and things. The Thursday the Catholic had their harvest, she was helping out as usual. Selling fry saltfish and bakes and making joke with everybody. The next morning early early we heard the person singing coming down the hill. At first we thought was McDowell, but when we listened we realised that it was a woman singing. I went by the road to see what was happening, only to see Miss Joycelyn well dress up in her church clothes, her bible and hymn book in her hand dancing and singing coming down the hill. When she reached the foreroad she started on about how the virgin Mary and the angel Gabriel visited her the night before and told her she must take up the cross and save the island from destruction. She went on and on like that for about a month. Not only was she preaching, but she was doing a lot of funny things as well. The neighbours couldn't sleep at nights the way she carried on . . . banging and shouting. The next thing was her family asked Dr Courtney to sign the papers to put her in Richmond Hill. They said it run in the family, because one of her brothers died in Richmond Hill and her mother was not all there in the head. Miss Joycelyn was funny in the head for true, but others who take up the bible had different reasons. As I said, I didn't know people went to school to learn to be priest. I thought they got the calling from God. Now I'm thinking perhaps is only Grenada people God does give the 'message'.

When the St. Lucian priest left, Father Jacob came. They said he was only recently ordained and this was his first parish church. At first everybody praised him. In Grand Roy,

Concorde and Happy Hill where he gave service, they all liked him. They said God send them another Father Gibbs. They almost worshipped the man. To tell the truth I used to be jealous of the Catholic children, with the things they were doing in their church and school. Father Gibbs always wanted to build a home for the old people. He bought the piece of land but did not get round to building; within nine months after Father Jacob came the home was ready for twelve old people to move in. In a way the two priest were very much alike. Although they were religious people, yet they knew how to handle the Government and get things done for the people in the villages. Before Aunty Floris went to Trinidad to live she had a small school up Mt. Nesbit road for about fourteen children about 3½ years old. Just Miss Moore used to do, Aunty Floris used to teach the children little ABC and to count their fingers. The place she used to keep the school wasn't good at all. Sometimes the children would be on her balcony, other times under her house. One day Father Jacob passed by her and noticed the crowd of children under the house. He stopped and asked what was happening. He and Aunty Floris had a long long talk. The result was he got the society people to agree to let Aunty Floris keep the school in the old society house. He also got carpenters and materials to fix up the place, even the latrine. All that, and Aunty Floris not even Catholic.

That was at first, then thing started happening. Little things, but people was talking about it. They started saying things like 'It's a pity such a nice young man not allow to have a wife.' Gossip started about how all kind of women in and out the rectory, saying is cleaning they cleaning. All kind of wayward boys sleeping there smoking and cursing all the time. The priest changed things around, even the choir practice. That started and later. Some parents stopped their children from going, especially the girls. Old members of the church like the Fergusons and the Johnsons went to talk to the priest, saying they worried about the reputation of the church. All the man said was all that talk was only gossip, not any truth in it at all. But things got worse. Soon people starting leaving the church, either to join other churches or to start their own religion. The Fergusons who were solid pillars left, but the strange thing was the same time they sent their daughter Annette to Trinidad on the quiet. One minute Annette was in the place happy, the next thing we hear she in Trinidad. Not a word to anybody that she going. I don't even think she told her best friend Sophia that she going, just up and gone. About a year later I hear people see her with a baby about three months old.

Some of these things I didn't understand, was Sheila who used to tell me what going on. I just listened and keep my mouth shut. Mammy would kill me if she catch me listening to big people business. Things went like that for about a year. The church was practically empty. Only Sheila still hot hot to go there. Is too much thing she have in she skin. Miss Chrissie and her husband was thinking of leaving as well, they had enough. Could be why Jane did what she did. You know, set trap to catch the priest in his nastiness. Still nobody ever thought she would actually slap the priest. Anyway it served him right, and as Mammy said Papa God would forgive her.

Miss Chrissie said she was surprised when Jane said she going to choir practice that day. They were worried too, especially when it was starting much later than usual. It was bad he changed the time from four in the afternoon to six, but then he changed that again to half past seven when outside dark. Was he and the devil planning their evil? He should of got more that a box. When I saw Mr Campbell in the police station, was complain he went and make to the police. He said if the police don't do anything about that savage they have in the church for priest, he making sure his cutlass well sharpen and hallelujah in the priest skin. The police said church business is not their business, but seeing how things were going one of them would go and talk to the man.

'Talk to him!' I hear Mr Campbell scrape his cutlass scruppe on the road. Fire spark from it. 'Talk to him! What you mean talk to him? The man interfering with people girl children; you sit down on you backside saying you go talk to him!' Mr Campbell was shaking as if he had spasm.

The corporal was frightened. Same time he sent a junior police to speak to the priest. Well, I hear in Africa they would beat the drums to send message from one village to the other. In Grenada they don't beat drum, but Lord talk about bush radio. It was still only early morning but by the time the police got to the rectory the man had all his things packed ready to move. We never found out how the bishop in town hear about what happened the night before so quick, but he ordered the young man to pack up and leave immediately. We think it was secret secret talk that went on between the bishop and old Catholic heads in the village. Anyway by midday Father Jacob left the place. Was a shame though. He did some good work for everybody around.

Some of the girls who used to go to choir practice and knew what went on started cursing Jane, saying was jealous she jealous. She think she this, she think she that. They too stupid. They picked on the wrong person. Jane don't trouble people, she walk was if her eyes are always closed, but you better don't mash her big toe. About three weeks after all that caca-cocoa, Sonia, that Miss Bayne daughter, take she farseness and stop Jane in the road. She run her mouth, run her mouth. Jane don't study her. She didn't get any satisfaction so she decided to square up in front Jane, letting her spit fly in the girl face. That day sun hot for so. Not a mountain breeze, not sea breeze blowing. The weather matched Jane's temper. Sonia say she hot like guinea pepper, that day she met her breaker. When Jane finished with her 'shame' didn't want her. Jane usually beat anybody with her tongue, not bad word or anything like that. Just tell you exactly what is what. If it comes to fighting with her hand, well . . . hand, head, foot everything join in. When she finished with Sonia, that girl belt down the bay road to her mother you would think Satan was behind her. Everybody said to Jane to run home and tell her mother what happened, because they were sure that Sonia gone for her mother, and they know that the woman don't have any reason for her children.

One day Mr George catch the boys stoning his mango, when he speak to them the smaller one pull down his trousers for the old man. Mr George went and complain to the mother. She listened, saying how sorry she was. Then she called the boys inside. Next thing you hear . . . blap, blap, plap, plaw, lick flying, and Miss Bayne quarrelling. The same time the little wind blow the curtain. When Mr George peep inside was the mattress the woman beating. Mind you, he lucky she didn't curse him. She don't have any reason at all, that's why everybody told Jane go home to her mother, because they expected Miss Bayne to come and let go her tongue. Jane just stand under the balcony, folded her arms waiting. About half hour afterwards she went home.

That afternoon Miss Bayne found her way to Jane's house. Miss Chrissie heard all that had happened earlier on from her

41

daughter. She wasn't surprised when she saw the woman coming up in the yard.

'Good day Miss Bayne,' Miss Chrissie said, meeting at the foot of the step leading into the house.

'Lawd dat sun hat you know! The tree and dem like they burning up,' Miss Bayne said.

'Is so; it stay in the dry season. We used to it. Still we could do with a little rain.' Miss Chrissie stick her eyes in the woman face waiting for her to say why she come. The same time Jane was coming from Rose, passing in the back yard. Although this morning she waited for the woman after the fight, now in the present of her mother she was a bit frightened. As soon as Miss Bayne saw her she called her.

'Jane, chile. Is you I come to see, yes.' Jane walked behind and stood next to her mother looking at the other woman. 'Chile I hear what happened this morning,' she continued. Jane started to tremble a little as she looked at her mother.

'Miss Bayne is Sonia started it you know,' Jane tried to explain.

'I know she start it. I always telling her about that badjohn she playing.' Jane looked at her mother, her mouth opened. Her mother looked at her, her lips pammed. They could not believe what they were hearing. When Jane told her mother what happened, her mother cautioned her about getting into bacanal with people like Sonia. Although she knew Jane don't take stupidness from anybody she still cautioned her, because everybody know Miss Bayne reputation. She was praying that she saw the woman before she meet up Jane in the road. Jane might forget herself and give her a piece of her tongue, and the other thing Mr Johnson would be involved. He would stand aside and let anybody assault his family. All

42

morning she worried about that. It seemed as if she worried for nothing.

'Eh, em,' Miss Bayne cleared her throat. 'I don't know what to do with the girl. I sorry for what happened. I tell Sonia she shouldn't behave like that. Told her the priest was no good and she mustn't go cussing decent people for him. I really sorry chile. It won't happen again, eeeem. Miss Chrissie I going by the bay, if I get anything I go send something for you . . . aright!' With that she made her way back to the main road.

Shock registered on Miss Chrissie and Jane's face. For a few minutes all they did was watched the back of the woman going down the road. When she was out of sight Jane burst out one laugh. She just couldn't believe what just happened. The only thing she could do was laugh.

The rectory stayed closed for weeks after that. Nobody don't know what happening. Mr Fitz the caretaker had the keys, so he used to open up the church and the rectory for people to go and pray. On one or two Sundays Mr Duncan kept a kind of mass. The worse part was the people who had their children to christen and Mildred already had her banns arranged to start reading for her wedding. Hot, hot brango started breaking out about all what really used to go on. One day I heard Mammy and Miss Chrissie talking about the state of the church. Apparently all the things that used to happen on the choir practice came out. Two of the girls' parents want to make a prayer for them for drinking the consecrated wine, and they didn't even make first communion yet. Lawd when Mammy and Miss Chrissie start to beat mouth, they go on and on for hours. Miss Chrissie must be Mammy best friend because is only home she does spent a some time, and sometimes Mammy pass her. They would

43

sit on the verandah for ages, sand flies and mosquito eating them up. Clap plaw, clap, plap, you hear them slapping mosquito, but that don't stop them. They accustomed to that.

3

In Grenada if mosquito don't bite you, something wrong with your blood. That's the thing with Grenada, the place nice nice and quiet, hot sun beating you every day. Even in the rain season when God decide to wash away Grenada sins, the sun does still be hot hot. There no body running, running to go anyway. Everything just slow and nice. Not like some people I see coming from England and America. These people always running as if they have pougatae in they skin. No wonder so many of them die of cardiac arrest. They run out their heart string. Sometimes they take their farse self and say how we slow like we don't have nothing to do. That make me really vex you know. Some of the tourist they come here wanting to draw pictures and things of people doing their work, like when Mammy and Miss Chrissie in the market selling their things. I tell Mammy she must turn her back, don't let them draw her picture. They come to Grenada enjoy all good things we have, then turn round and say we slow and lazy. When a little sandfly bit them they start bawling.

One day I tell Sheila I feel like catching a centipede and letting it go by them when they in town. Sheila started to laugh.

'How you go catch centipede Flora?' she asked.

'How you mean how I go catch it? How you think?'

Sheila laughed even more. I thought she was being stupid. I didn't see anything to laugh about.

'Flora Williams!' she said. Hands on her waist like a big woman. Her eyes poking in my face. 'Flora Williams, how you think you go catch centipede to put by anybody when you 'fraid the beast like cat 'fraid holy water? Eh? How?!'

I had to laugh. Is true. I see one little centipede and I bawl all kind of bawl. But these people . . . I tell you. The way they get on if a little sandfly bite them you would think is the end of the world. I don't know what they would do if they boot up on a serpent or even a big creeboe. I would like to know. Then again, perhaps they would like that, because I hear that these American and English people funny. I hear they keep serpent and snakes inside their house for pets. Even dog and cat eating and sleeping inside their house. These people must be mad.

Well Mammy and Miss Chrissie was talking about the christening that was supposed to take place in the church soon. I remember all these things at teacher wedding. Not that it had anything to do with it, only after teacher wedding there is christening as well. You should of seen Father Bernard face when teacher grandmother bawled out. I'm sure he thought that Satan was about to take over his church. It look as if Satan had a habit of always popping up in church. What Miss Chrissie was saying was now that Father Jacob gone, everything in confusion. No priest, and even the church wine gone missing. The godparents for Daisy child came from Trinidad with the cake and everything. When they see time getting near and no priest they took the child in Brizan where her other godmother lived and christened

46

her there. That was alright, but the wedding was confusion. Everything was prepared. The bridesmaid clothes, the food for the fête . . . everything. A lady in town was making the wedding cake. When I heard that I thought to myself . . . I hope is not Miss Laqua. Cars and flowers were arranged; but no priest. They went and asked the priest in Victoria but he said he can't do it without permission from the bishop. In the end they went to ask the bishop, and he send a priest from Grenville. When they hear a priest was coming, everybody who had a child to christen in Catholic rush rush to get the child christened, because nobody knew when priest would come again. Shirley's child father was fattening a goat for his child christening the month after. The godmother who was looking after the cake was about to go to Trinidad for a couple of weeks. In the end Shirley had the child christened without the fête. When they came from the church they only had a glass of wine to wet the baby's head and arranged the fête for the next month. One ruction to get the church cleaned up in time. It's a good thing I didn't take my farseness and asked Mammy to send me there when Sheila was behind me to join them.

I don't know; this place so small but the things that happen is enough. Still it's the best place in the world to live. People go away to big countries for years; when they come back they still say how nice the island is. It's not only Grand Roy and the other villages around; it's the whole of Grenada. Everything quiet. Even when people cursing and bad mouthing each other. It's kind of nice . . . Even when the people in Government House don't know what they doing and arguing with each other . . . it's all part of life. It's always nice and quiet. I say quiet, but sometimes when the big trucks tumbaying down the hill . . . a dooop, dooop, booop, boop, as if they bringing the whole of Marigot down in the foreroad.

Our home is sort of sandwiched between the mountain and the sea. When it's really hot the breeze from the mountain and the sea helps to cool the place a bit. Being more or less on the coast, the main road from Sauteurs to St. Georges passes through the village. The road narrow, narrow like snake belly. It's like one long silver-black snake coiling in and out . . . slitty, slittering up a little hill, down a dip. Sometimes between thick provision and fruit trees. Travelling from Palmiste to Gouyave although you on the main road in between provision, you still near the sea. Whether you walking or driving, you could look down into the sea water and see little fishes swimming about. If the sea is rough the waves wash right in the road. Anybody passing have to time the waves and run or get a good soaking. Say you going to Sauteurs by bus from St. Georges, it's like you doing all sort of dance in one. One minute the bus bend this way, next it twist the other way. Before you blink you eyes zuish, cruish, you flying up one hill then jukotoo juk you rolling down another. One minute you by the sea, the next you in the bush belly, and you still travelling along the same main road. For instance, once you cross Grand Roy bridge and go around Boawden corner, it's the sea to left and rocks and thick provision and things on the other side, even over your head.

In the rain season the rock is covered in nice beautiful green clothes. All sort of vines twist itself to form a hot blanket. The vines are all sorts. There are fruit vines like the nice juicy yellow water lemon. Nobody take notice of it until they start riping and falling in the road. There is the stinking-toe. Same as the water lemon, you don't know the tree is

48

between the vine until the hard-shelled fruit start to fall. Not everybody like stinking-toe, they say it make news like manderin. The shell is as hard as coconut so you have to take a stone to pound it open. If you not careful, all the dry powder inside fly up in your face and on your clothes. Even when you eating it, it makes news. Once it's in your mouth, it feels like wet flour, sticky sticky, and messing up your face. Not only that but the name describe it just right . . . because it smells strong. Apart from fruit vines we also get skipping rope between the bushes.

If someone wants to really enjoy a nice refreshing walk along the sea front early morning is the best time. That's the time when the sea breeze cool and refreshing, and as the birds would be getting up to hear them singing is just wonderful. A stranger taking a walk would find it hard to believe it's one main road that runs all round the island. It branches off all over the place like centipede legs, but you can still follow the one road. If you in Grand Roy and walking, to, say, past Victoria, when you leave Boawden gap, walk across Lapoutree to White Gate and you'll pass under the big silk cotton tree. People afraid to walk there in the night; they say in the trunk is the devil and his disciples' workshop. I don't believe all that stupidness. I more believe it's the owners of the gardens behind the tree that trying to frighten people to prevent them from thiefing their food and things, especially the fruits. Right by the side of the tree is a big mango Rose tree. When it's in season the owner hardly get one mango to make remedy. School children stoning the mango, even before they start to ripe.

There are plenty of other fruits as well. Lots of guava trees. When they riping and the sun hot, the sweet smell of those big yellow guava hit your nose like essence. Sometimes it smell as if guava jelly or cheese cooking. The thing with guava is not only children love it, but snakes too. You see a tree branches spread out covered in juicy yellow guava, then you notice holes in the fruits. When you look closer you have to run because what you see is a long silver snake sliding and twisting among the branches. It move about just like the bus on the road, in and out around and about. One minute the head is one place, next minute it's on another branch and you hardly notice it moving. They say the snakes are not dangerous. They reckon it is more afraid of people than the other way round, but I'm not going close to find out, especially if the sun splitting earth. Some stories have it that in the heat the snakes get vex and fly.

Not only in the guava trees snakes live but in the silk cotton tree as well . . . snakes and great big black and white, and sometimes red, serpents. They twist up, twist up around the branches of the silk cotton tree. Could be why they believe the devil and his disciples are happy there. Some of the things you hear is really hard to believe. Sometimes again it's hard not to think about them, because for instance look how the silk cotton tree shape. It shaped different from the other trees. It sort of stands like a house on four posts, and boarded up on three sides with a door on the fourth side. It's the tallest and biggest tree along the road. The trunk is big and thick, not like a big mango tree or anything like that. If you peep inside it's like a big dark room. The branches spread wide all around like a umbrella, covering the road and over the sea. Its shadow shades straight out to the big white stone in the middle of the water.

That's another thing. They say that a mermaid lives under the stone. Certain time of the year in the middle of the night on a full moon night she would come out and sit on the

50

stone combing her long hair. She always sit with her back to the road. Nobody ever saw her face clearly. She sits in a way that only the top part of her body is out of the water.

Mammy told me a story that happened a long time ago. It's a long time but the man is still alive. He in the poor house in Mileweze now. His sister is old living somewhere in Shantimel. Anyway, Mammy said one Friday night moonlight bright a gang of young boys were walking from Victoria to home. They stayed liming in Victoria until it late and they couldn't get a lift, so they decided to walk. As they got near to the silk cotton tree they smelt that sweet sweet perfume. Nice lady perfume. Because of all the stories they know about the place, smelling perfume this time of the night was something to make the hair in their head raise up. Caryle started shaking like a leaf. Same time he grabbed Matthew hand saying, 'O gawd boy. You smell it. Mus be lajabless going home. We done tonight . . . we done.' They were about to run when Amos noticed a shadow on the stone.

'Aaye; all you look. Look. I think is the merrimaid perfume. Look she on the stone.' He shouted out. Stand up plamp under the silk cotton tree.

'What you on about man?' Cecil shouted to him. 'Come on run . . . run.'

'Look . . . Look!' Amos pointing to the stone. 'I always hearing about the merrimaid, I never see her. Is six of us; she can't do us anything.'

'Amos, Amos you stupidy,' Matthew shouted. 'Come on before she get you. Amos, come on.' Amos took no notice of his friends. He was fascinated by the figure on the stone. He stood on the narrow wall separating the road from the

51

sea, still pointing to the figure. The shadows of the leaves were like dancers on his face.

'Look; all you look. The moon bright I could see her good good. It's the mermaid alright. You all too damn coward. I want to see her legs.' Amos started to jump behind the wall.

'Amos you idiot! Come back. She don't have legs. Amos, come back. She don't have legs, she have fish tail,' Caryle shouted.

'Yeh, what leg. You ever hear merrimaid have legs? You can't even see her face properly. You think is her legs you go see,' Cecil added. 'Come on, let's run.' The young men had moved from under the shadow of the tree and were limbering between a brisk walk and full scale run.

'Is woman you want. Go on, is woman you after.'

Gordon who was quiet all the while added. 'You smell sweet perfume in the middle of the night. You see merrimaid sitting on the stone for you to run like hell. You on about you going to see her legs, you good day oui!' With that last remarks the boys started to run. A now excited Amos was foot searching for safe place to approach the beach to have a closer look. The last thing the other boys saw of him was the shadow of his white jersey half way on the shore like a spirit.

About half past three the next morning Miss Mina wake up to get her things ready to go to the market. She expected Amos to get up when he hear her in the kitchen. She busy busy in the kitchen, packing the baskets and things. No Amos. This boy so lazy, she muttered to herself. 'He so damn lazy. Last night he go and wet his tail in Victoria, this morning he can't get up to help me.'

She went around the house to his room. Opened the door, pushed her head towards the corner where his bed is. 'Amos,' she called quietly, not wanting to wake his sister in the next room. 'Amos, time to get up.' No answer. She went inside and was about to pull the cover when she noticed that the bed hadn't been slept in. Everything was just as she left it when she made up his bed yesterday morning.

Miss Mina started quarrelling, saying how Amos is a good for nothing. He know is Saturday morning and his father not home. The boy knows that. He knows his father still in Trinidad. These Trinidad people is something else. Always mashing up people business. All the time for them to strike they don't strike. They wait until the nutmeg co-operation meeting finish and the people have to come back to Grenada to close down Piarco airport. Now the man can't come home until Sunday morning. Amos knows that . . . he knows; you know. Instead of coming home to help to bring the load by the road and go in the bush early to change the animal he following woman frock tail. She was real vex, but something inside her sort of telling her something else, as if some body trying to talk to her. She went back inside the room and looked around. Nuh, something wrong. Something wrong, she thought. She shook her head. 'Mavis, Mavis get up,' she called her daughter. 'Get up girl, you brother didn't come home last night.' She went to the girl's room. 'Amos! Mavis you hear me girl, get up. You hear what I say. Amos didn't come home last night.'

Mavis was four years younger than Amos, but since Amos came to live with them after their grandmother died, they were very close. If Amos meant to sleep out he would tell his sister. He usually tell her most things he did in the village. When she heard her brother didn't come home, Mavis jumped out of her sleep as if she was pushed out of a dream.

'You brother tell you nuthing yesterday?' her mother ask. 'He tell you he go sleep out last night?'

'No Ma'am. What you mean?' Mavis was wondering about the girl up the road that Amos told her about. He better be careful. These people and them don't make joke with their girl children, you know.

'What you mean, what I mean? I tell you he din sleep in his bed.'

'Amos don't sleep out, Ma. Perhaps he went to the garden early.'

'Nuh, girl something wrong. His garden clothes hang up on the nail.' Miss Mina stood in front of Amos room, one hand crossed in front her, the other cupped her mouth. Her piercing eyes seemed to be boring into the door. Mavis came out to meet her. It was then about four o'clock.

'Don't worry Ma'am, he soon come. Perhaps they sleep in Victoria, he soon come.'

The same time they heard footsteps on the gravel in the front yard. Mavis laugh, 'See what I tell you? You wake me up for nothing. I tell you he soon come.'

'Amos. Amos,' a voice called in the front yard. Quick quick Miss Mina followed by Mavis went to see who it was. Outside was still dusky. They could just make out Caryle standing like a spirit in front the door.

'Caryle, whey Amos?' Miss Mina asked. 'I thought he went out with you last night, eh? Whey him? He din sleep in his bed last night.'

'Marning Miss Mina,' the young man said.

'Whey's Amos?' Mavis asked.

In the half darkness he looked even darker than usual. He started scratching. His hands went to his head, then his foot, then to his back.

'Caryle, where is Amos?' Mavis asked again, seeing his movement. 'What wrong with you?'

'I thought he came home, Miss Mina. I thought he came home. That's why I come and call him to go in the bush.' Caryle was jumpy as if jumbie was playing with him.

Miss Mina was not actually looking at the young man. She was looking at his dim shadow doing a sort of African war dance as he scratched himself.

'Amos didn't come home,' Mavis said. 'What was the last time you see him last night? You all left him in Victoria, eh Caryle? You left him in Victoria last night didn't you?'

'O Gawd Bunjay oye,' Caryle bellowed. With that, before Mavis or Miss Mina can open their mouth, he turned and run towards his home. The day was beginning to brighten up. The reflection of the sun was over the mountain. The neighbours were getting up. Miss Mina heard Mr Baptiste talking in his house. She called him and tell him that Amos did not come home last night. She babbled on what happened a few minutes ago, but Mr Baptiste was not listening.

'Perhaps he find a young lady in Victoria,' he joked.

She went and stand behind her kitchen where she can see Mr Baptiste in front his door. She related again the incident with Caryle a few minutes ago.

'True. I saw them going up last night. Was Amos, Cecil, Caryle and Eddie two boys. Did Caryle say where they left Amos, or where he was when they last saw him?'

'The boy din say nuthing. Just started bawling for papa bunjay and running. Mr Baptiste, someting happen to Amos. Someting funny happen to my boy. I going in the police station.'

'I coming Ma'am. I coming,' Mavis said.

Mr Baptiste left his wife preparing the tea saying he going

to the police station with the neighbour. By that time Miss Mina was half way down the road, her two hands on her head bawling, and Mavis behind her also bawling. By the time they reach the station Caryle was there dancing like he had pougatae in his skin. Although it was very early morning people was by the road, already wondering what's happening. Miss Marcia, that's Eddie's wife, came and hold up Miss Mina. Cecil's mother and father was there. Cecil behind them looking like a spirit. Miss Mina and Mavis bawling how something happened to Amos, without even knowing anything at all. How the rumour reach up Mt. Plaisir so quickly no body knows, but Amos aunty, the one he couldn't get on with, she come running down the road screaming how they kill her nephew.

In the confusion that followed, the police managed to get a story from Cecil and Caryle. Some people found it very funny . . . they couldn't understand how Amos could be so stupid . . . or why the other boys didn't drag him home. But then some said the mermaid already had Amos marked out, there was nothing anyone could do. A group of men decided to go and look for the boy. Miss Mina wanted to go with them, but they told her to stay in the station. Mavis stayed with her but her aunt went with the men. When they reached around Boawden corner they saw some of the bay men coming towards them. The way they were shouting and waving their hands it was obvious they were not talking about fish. Three men were sort of carrying a bundle. It was Amos. Apparently after the men from Allen cast their net, the lookout man spotted a person sort of folded up between the stone hole under the silk cotton tree. He called out, but the person did not answer. He then shouted to the others on the shore. That's how they found Amos, naked apart from

56

his tear up jersey in his hand. All what they asked him the only thing he kept saying was: 'She prutty, prutty prutty.' That was hot hot news for a few weeks. They teased Amos, teased Amos. They even made carnival song on him. After a while, people don't bother with him. He was just there saying nothing but: 'She prutty prutty prutty.' One thing for sure, for a long time those boys never stayed in Gouyave late.

Even now, people say when they pass under the tree you could smell either sweet sweet woman perfume or strong medicine like a doctor shop.

When you leave from under the silk cotton tree you approach Palmiste beach. At a glance, all you see is the sea and a stretch of grey white sand with a coconut-tree lining. The road disappears to reappear again about half a mile ahead on a little hill under Mango Palmer. It look as if you only have to walk straight across the sand to be on the hill, but then you will be missing the big estate house with its large open gate, where, if you are lucky to, could get a glimpse of the workers putting out the fresh cocoa seeds to dry or bringing in freshly cut bunches of green bananas in preparation for shipping.

There are few houses along that stretch of road, only one or two like Miss Julie and her family who lived at the end of the long row of coconut trees. The road to the estate house is like everywhere else, twisting and winding like a snake. It's strange, although it seemed that you have been walking for a long time yet you are not really tired. The sun by then would be high over the mountain but the sea air is still cool. When you leave the estate you come to Mt. Nesbit bay house. You can sit on the sea wall and lazily watch the waves splish splashing on the beach, or if you are feeling adventurous you can take a paddle among the tiny waves as they lash on the shore. It could also be your lucky day when the fishermen are casting their nets. The rhythm of bodies and voices as they oyoye-hey-hep-ahepoyoy is temptation to join in. You could be rewarded with fresh fish for breakfast. From Mt. Nesbit bay on to 'Mango Palmer'. This is a cluster of big mango trees on both sides of the road which forms an arch where the workers and travellers rest from the hot sun. Between there and the cemetery house on Douglastone Bridge there is not a house in sight. Could be why there are so many funny stories about the place. Stories like it's where those bad men usually hide when police after them. Apparently they hide under the bushes and between the rocks.

When I first started going to school in Gouyave there was a bad bad man in Victoria. They say he used to hide under these bushes. I don't know how true this is. I never see him. I used to walk that road almost every day, going to church and then when I started to go to Gouyave school. Only once or twice I remember anything frightened me around there. The first time when I told Mammy she said is coward, we damn coward. She said was our mind that frightened us, but I know what I saw . . . it was right in the middle of the road. I know I'm a coward, but there was big people there as well . . .

We were walking home from midnight mass on Christmas Eve. Only one bus came up that night, and that was full up of Roman Catholic people. The moon was bright like foreday morning, so Miss Cochrane and the other big people said we could walk home. We were chatting, laughing and singing Christmas carol as we strolled under Mabouya to Mango Palmer. Me, Magna and James was a little way in front the others. As we rise out of the dip we saw it. I think I saw it

58

first. I don't remember. I grabbed Magna hand so hard is a good thing she strong. The same time James sort of move closer to me as if he trying to disappear in me. The three of us hold hands and back back to the others. We didn't say anything, just pointed to this thing in the middle of the road. At first I could not make out what it was. Everybody was quiet. All eyes on this big, white dog sitting stiff stiff in the middle of the road, that time of the morning. It sat there back towards the sea and head looking straight up at the mango tree . . . not a twich . . . not a blink. I'm sure it heard us, but did not move . . . not a bit. We walked quick quick in the bush behind it. Everybody quiet. As we passed it, Mr George shouted out something in patois. Magna started to laugh because she understood what he said. I did not know much of that language. When I go to my grandmother she used to teach me one one words. She always say I should learn to speak two tongues. Sometimes I get confused because my grandmother wants me to learn patois but when we at Aunt Sar and Tanty Mildred they only speak the language when they don't want children to understand what they were saying. If we hang around to try to pick up one one word they threaten to beat us, saying we too farse in big people business. I learned a few words but when people speak too quickly like Mr George did I don't understand them. Anyway, after we passed the dog we glanced back, and there was nothing there, just nothing. Mammy said is my mind that frightened me. I don't know if she would say it was Mr George mind as well. When I said that she said perhaps the dog owner was hiding in the mango tree. Perhaps he was thiefing and when he heard us coming he went and hide. That doesn't explain why the dog sat there stiff stiff as a statue. That was one time I was frightened along that road.

I think we better move on from under Mango Palmer to Mabouya rock. This place has a history of itself. I suppose everybody who ever walked that road had some kind of story. To write about everything would be a history book in itself. The piece of road between the big boucanoe tree and the clump of grapefruit trees is a Government headache. The road dip down in a deep hole. Always sinking. No matter the amount of repairs the Government repair, it still sinks. Men came from Canada and America to find out why, one time they said there was a spring running underneath, so they dig deep deep and try to block it up with concrete. As soon as they full up the holes what happen? The road sink deeper. They tried to cut another one just over where the worse part was; as soon as they started that started sinking too. I'm sure the Government spend most of their road money trying to fix Mabouya road. The strange thing is in the dry season it's worse. I don't know. Anyway for about half a mile it's as if you are walking in the heart of the forest and on the beach at the same time.

The road sort of runs inside the belly of stools of bananas, sprinkled with countless fruit trees – oranges, grapefruit, mangoes, almond – all sort. In between you find a nutmeg tree laden with opened or half opened pods. The opened pods are like light pink lips slightly opened exposing the red mace and hard brown shell that encase the nutmeg itself. A cocoa tree covered with yellow fruit and the occasional sugar cane stalk adds to the natural tapestry. A crick, and a crack may disclose a donkey, lazily grazing beneath the twisting vines, or the bow bowing of a dog as it chases a manicou or mongoose. Everything merges into each other. The exotic mingled fragrance is like fermented alcohol. Inhale too long and you'll sure be drunk. With all that around you still only have to peep between the dancing leaves to your left to glimpse the twinkling starlike bluey-silvery waves of the sea.

Move on to history itself. The amazing rock – Mabouya. The sheer white rock precipitously overlooking the stretch of beach below. Apart of stories of strange devil happening under the rock, there are disaster tales. Many people have lost their lives there, either by vehicle running off the road into the sea below or by loose boulders escaping on to someone.

At last Douglastone Bridge is in sight – the gateway to the ancient town of Gouyave. The narrow road continues across the bridge with the cemetery overlooking the park into the town. Then on to Victoria, then Sauteurs where you might care to visit 'Leapers Hill' the place where the last of the Caribs, about forty in number, ended their lives instead of surrendering to French. Then on to LaBaye, Birchgrove, over the hills or around St. Davids to St. Georges and along the western side back to Grand Roy. All the way the narrow road slitters on. Legs spring off here and there, leaving the 'mother' to go on her way.

> Twisting, bending,
> from St. Georges to Mount Gay,
> New Hampshire to Vendomme.
>
> Twisting, bending, gliding,
> smoothly, bumpy, holey
> on and on and on.
>
> Like a silver congaree,
> looping, hooping, up and over the hills
> through Grand Etang's evergreen nursery
> to Birchgrove to Grenville.

Gliding, sliding, twisting, bending,
from St. Georges to Perseverance
to Concorde, Grand Roy, Gouyave and
Victoria, completing the western route to
Sauteurs.

Twining, twisting, looping
up down around and around,
twisting, turning,

hooping, slittering, gliding,
like a silvery-grey congaree-legged snake
in slow motion, the narrow main road winds
on and on and on.

The road rolls on with the pace of everything.

4

Nothing in a hurry. Everything just cool, slow and nice. Everybody going about their business in their own time. Even when they minding other people business, they not in a hurry. Grenada people always laughing and friendly, even when badmouthing and cursing each other. It's sort of confusion and not confusion.

Tourist always saying how they love the island. Some come for their holidays in Grenada every year. One woman from Canada comes every year for about six years, every time she come she brings friends with her. She says Grenada holds a sort of fascination for her; the atmosphere and character of the island. She became very friendly with those Louisons in the big house behind the Catholic church, so when she comes on holiday now she don't go to hotel, she stays with them. I heard her say something once, made me really vex. When she come here, well not only her, but people from overseas, especially those from cold countries, they walk as if they had police behind them, fast, fast, fast. I used to think maybe in their country they had to be always running to prevent snow from sipping underneath their skull, or perhaps they had snow inside their heads. Anyway I heard her say that Grenadians walk as if they don't have anything to do. The way she said it sounded as if she mean lazy, we lazy. I tell you, if she wasn't a big woman I would of tell her something, stranger or no stranger. Because we don't run as if we have zoutee in our skin don't mean we don't work hard for a living. Nobody work harder than Mammy and Miss Chrissie and her husband. I don't know what they want us to do. The place hot, hot. We must be mad to run about in the heat for our heart string to burst.

The only time people move about quickly is carnival time. Then everybody ready for a good jump up. Even those people who go to church and pray three times a week, come carnival they right in the jump up. After that come Ash Wednesday they go back to church for ashes and ask God to forgive them. Mammy say is hypocrite, some of them hypocrite. Fancy doing something deliberately and then going and ask God to forgive you. Still is not everybody that play mas. For one thing Mammy don't play, and she don't let me play. She don't mind me standing by the road with my friends and watching what going on, as long as I don't go and jump up. I still enjoy myself, though.

I remember one jouvere morning when I was little. The usual thing on the Sunday night before carnival Monday morning, people hardly sleep. Most of them who playing mas would make big fête. Sometimes they go way up in the mountain, sometimes they stay just under the cocoa by the river. Weeks before carnival they usual hunt in the night for manicou or tattoo and corn it for the fête on the Sunday night, then they would cook the meat with big stiff dumpling and pease. Sometimes split pease, sometimes green pigeon pease. With that they would also cook rice and provision. When Uncle Andrew used to play steel band with Alan and some others, they used to cook by the river under Mr Black piece of cocoa and the Monday morning he would bring a big calabash full of food for us. I used to like that, especially those big dumpling. When you bite them they go 'keeks'.

Anyway, that particular Monday morning, about three o'clock, people started blowing shell, phew, pheew all down the bay road, then up Mt. Plaisir road some body started beating an old kerosene pan. I lie in bed trying to sleep. Although I love carnival, two things I 'fraid is old mas and the devil mas. Anyway, early early they started making noise. I decided to stay in my bed until sun rise because I not going and watch no old mas. About half past four there was one bacanal in our gap. A clack a tang, clack a tang, bang a lang bang, one ruction in the gap. I peep through the little hole, in the board under the window by my bed, to see what was making that noise. This time Mammy was already up and in the kitchen, making the tea and breakfast, so although I couldn't see anything I was really frightened. There was another bang a lang bang, ding ding, clack a clack, and this somebody was shouting. I peeped in the hole again, and saw this old mas coming up in our yard. I wanted to pee but I wasn't getting up. The devil mas could be some-body you know good, but the way he paint up himself shinning greasy black, and his mouth rouge up red red. He even put stuff on his fingernails – they long long as if is pieces of old pan they stick on with old gooseberry, and that's painted red as well. Inside the eyes red as when people making lougarou. The whole body like it rub down with charcoal mixed with vaseline. They hardly wear any clothes, sometimes only a little piece of pants covering their front and bottom. The worse part of the whole thing is the basket or bag that they carry. These men really nasty, you know. I don't know how they could take their hands and catch these big old beasts. I mean in the bag they carry big serpent or snake and threaten to throw it on who don't give them any money.

As I said, them and old mas are the ones that really frighten me. That old mas that was coming in front our door that morning was dressed in strings . . . bits of strings hanging his body. On his head was the rim of an old straw hat, even that was tied up with fig string. His shoes was fig leaves tied up with skipping rope. When I saw him standing on the step in front our door I pelt my head deep back under the sheet, and kept quiet. I felt the pee wetting my panty but I wasn't getting up. The funny thing was that all that time Mammy in the kitchen not saying a word. Well not at first. Was as if she didn't hear anything. Then I heard her laughing. Imagine old mas right in front the door and Mammy laughing, and to make matters worse I heard somebody calling my name. At first I thought that it was fright made me hearing things, but he called me again. Called in a sort funny funny voice, as when we taking out nancy story and trying to talk like Anancy. Well I tell you, whoever calling could call until first cock crow next morning, I not going out there. A few minutes things was a bit quiet, I only could hear the old pan clang clanging each other. Then Mammy came inside and called me. Telling me to come and see something outside. She shake me, shake me because she thought that I was sleeping.

'Flora, aye aye what do you girl?' I didn't answer.

'Flora, old mas up and down the road, you still lie down sleeping. Aaye what do you? Get up, nuh! What do you?'

'Nuthing.' I muffled from under the sheet.

'Get up girl, somebody calling you outside.'

By this time I was lying in a little spot of pee. I pushed

my head from under the cover to look at Mammy. First thing I noticed was her eyes – they were laughing. Her big brown eyes were laughing as when the sun just come up over the mountain after a heavy shower of rain. I squinted my eyes to make sure it was Mammy. It was my mother alright, and not only her eyes were laughing but her whole face. The broad nose, the luscious thick lips that sometimes look thinner when she pammed them together, her whole beautiful brown face was laughing. Mammy is always a cheerful person, always with a smile or ready for a laugh, but that morning there was something new about her laughing face. I kept squinting at her from under the cover. I still didn't trust to come out.

'Get up girl, somebody calling you outside,' she repeated.

I looked at her again. She had a piece of rag in her hand. It was a piece of cloth from her old flowered cotton dress she used to go in the garden with. Something started puzzling my mind. I peeped outside again at the old mas. Pieces of the rags he had around him was from the same old dress as the piece in Mammy hand. Then it clicked. The week before my Uncle Andrew asked Mammy for some old rags. She tore up the skirt of her old dress and gave the pieces to him. I thought he wanted it to tie up in his garden to scare away the birds and monkeys from his corn. I pushed the sheet from over me. Mammy was really laughing now. She was sitting on the edge of my bed laughing. I'm not sure whether she was laughing at the mas or at me . . . she was just laughing with long water running down her face. Just imagine my own uncle frightening me.

That is how it is with carnival. Some people disguise them to play old mas, others join bands, some again just do their thing. Sometimes it's real surprising to find out who that

67

particular mas is. Carnival is usually the Monday and Tuesday before Ash Wednesday, so it's the last bash before the Lent season. It's not surprising to find the Sunday School teacher playing mas. Lent season is really hot season. Sometimes you think the sun is having a special bash as well during carnival. Somehow the hot sun adds an extra zooom to the whole thing. As I said, most of the people who playing in a band don't sleep on Sunday night, they go fêting . . . eating food and drinking old 'LaSagesse' and making noise. Since before first cock crow the noise start . . . bell, shell, old pan, old hoe, cutlass anything that can make a noise . . . bang pang, ding ling, bow oye oyoye ohoye . . . all kind of noises plus people mouth.

There was another carnival Monday morning when Mr Benson from over the river was ringing his bell . . . clackatang, clang clang, clack atang, ding ding. 'People oye!' he shouted. 'People oye . . . Listen . . . Listen people. I must tell you that. I must tell you the whole world ended yesterday. People oye listen. England and America finished . . . True. The world ended yesterday. England and America finished.' Clang clang clang, a lang tang, he rang his bell.

That same evening Miss Peters, the Sunday school teacher in the Anglican church, was dressed up in her father old black suit. She walked up and down the road between the crowds. She also had on a pair of glasses frame and an old umbrella swinging on her arm. At first we did not know who it was because she painted on a beard and moustache. It was really funny.

The best one that year was when that person appeared in the middle of a 'jump up'. I say a person because in carnival you never sure if it's a man or woman, no matter how the person is dressed. Anyway, that Tuesday steel band hot, sun hot, calypso hot and everybody on fire . . . carnival fire. All of sudden, somebody shouted out at the top of their voice 'Woye o yoye, look at dat . . . woye o yoye.' This person was standing in the crowd like the queen of England . . . well like some queen or the other. She had on one of the loveliest long bright red dress I ever saw. If it was all white you would say she was getting married. The bodice of the dress was high neck and tight fitting. The front was covered with very fine white embroidered granny lace. In the waist there was a thin band leading down to a full flowing wide stiff skirt. The can can under the skirt made it as stiff as if there was bamboo underneath. The dress was long that you couldn't see the person's foot, not even the tip of the toe. The outfit was topped with a big, white wig and long white gloves. The white painted face finished the disguise. The whole thing was just beautiful, but it was the person inside the outfit that had everybody eyes popping out. 'She' was dancing. I mean dancing on one spot. All the shoving and pushing around her she did not move. She stood on that spot and shally, shimmer and shally. The hand on her waist, in the air. Shoulder shook left, then right. And as for her bottom, woye o yoye. She shook it over, brought it up, down, round and round. Hand, shoulder, head and bottom together they shally bop dop shilly shimmer in unison. All that without moving one step nor making a single sound. I tell you, everybody stopped to watch that person. Each beat of the steel band pan she move. Every 'woye' she move.

'Who is dat?' everybody asked. Nobody could guess. 'Aye aye look at that backside,' someone observed. 'Saye saye, I see,' another answered. 'But you don't see, she not moving at all,' another comment. 'Perhaps she have hoof for foot.'

And so the remarks continued. The person kept on dancing. Sometimes both hands brace the waist, with only moving part being the bottom and the belly. The next minute the shoulder, waist and head take over.

After a few minute there was a 'doop'. A single 'doop'. Yet enough to make an impression. Eyes rolled. Mouth opened. Doop, doop, plap, three steps, three short steps. At that someone in the crowd shouted out that you would think that it was the queen that was crowned. Doop, doop, doop, plap, the dancing figure moved. 'Bonjay oye,' Miss Eva screeched. 'Lawd, all you look at me trouble, nuh? All you doh know who dat.'

Doop, doop, doop, plap, doop. A doop, plap, doop, a doop, the dancing figure jigged, shallied, skimmered and jigged. Moving only the few steps in the crowd.

'Aaye but look at my trouble, nuh,' Mr Gifford echoed as he edged his way closer. 'This carnival is something, oui. Even Alice playing mas.' As if the performance was finished the dancing figure began to undress. She took off the gloves, then carefully unzipped the dress and slipped that down to the ground. She then straightened her everyday frock she had underneath. Then the wig came off. Every move she made, her shoulder, belly and bottom danced. Still wearing the mask she slowly stepped out of the dress. Lifting first her right foot, then in slow motion her wooden left foot. Lastly she whipped off the mask. 'Boy dis ting hat like fire,' she grinned. 'It make hat like hell.'

'Yeh, Alice, it hat like hell gal. Dis is carnival,' Mr Gifford added.

That's what it is like in Grenada. That's the time when everybody wake up to enjoy themselves on the road. There are fêtes and things all the time, but carnival time is different.

70

It's the whole island together doing things. The costumes, the bands, the acting history and things. Some of the songs the calypsonians make are about things that happen locally. Like when the mermaid turned Amos stupidy.

Even what happened at teacher wedding, if it was near carnival they would make song about it. I'm glad because it would not be fair to make song on people when it's not their fault. Nobody expected the old lady to get on like that at her granddaughter wedding.

Still she is nothing like Miss O'Brien. Calypsonian must be tired making song about her. The things you hear about this woman sometimes make you wonder if it's the same person. She is very old anyway. Must have about one hundred. Some of the things are hard to believe, but then the way me and Sheila saw her in the sea that day I can't help thinking that some are true. Mammy said the woman took after her mother. People say she catch mama malady from her mother. I don't see how that could happen. As far as my grandmother told me, if somebody have mama malady is because of something bad that happened to you, so I don't see how somebody else could catch it from you. They say there is a woman in LaFelette that have the sickness on her. They say this woman had ten children. Lawd imagine having ten children to cook and wash for. Is only me and Mammy now, and she bawling how I dirtying clothes and everyday her hand in water washing. Everyday she have to cook. Imagine if she had ten children to look after, especially when they are all little.

Anyway, the story was that the woman was making another baby and something funny happened because the baby was not a baby at all. When time for she to have the child, both of them died. According to Mammy she heard was the same thing that happened to Miss O'Brien mother. All that must of happened even before Mammy born. The story was that the woman was about 45 and making baby. To me that was too old for anybody to have baby. Everybody was surprised, because for one thing her husband died about five years before and the woman always preaching about how she is a good Christian woman. Everybody was running their mouth, how the woman is the devil; she preaching about God and doing the devil work. But Miss Eslyn had another story. She said it was God work. (Funny how people always blame God. Is always God this, God that. Never the devil, no matter how bad things are. It's always the same, even today. People working their nastiness and claiming is God work. Sometimes I think to myself that poor God must suffer from bad bad headache.) Anyway, more people run their mouth, the more Miss Eslyn on about how it was God child she making. She went on about how after she made so many children God send her a special child to look after her in her old age. All the church people got vex. They told her not to take God name in vain. Mammy said the woman must of been an old stupidy to think she could fool people. Even Jesus had a mother and father. Things got so bad that everybody stopped speaking to the woman, even stop their children from playing with her children. Apparently something was wrong, because after nine months the baby still didn't born. People started calling the woman elephant. People really wicked, you know. The woman must of been well sick; instead of trying to help her they bad mouthing her.

People started saying is not real baby in her belly. They even said that perhaps it's an old snake or something like that. Lawd people real stupid, imagine saying snake in somebody belly. While the people calling her elephant and saying is obeah, she work that back fired, the woman was suffering. That went on for about fourteen months until the doctors found out that it was a growth in her belly and not baby. The doctor wanted to operate but she said she not letting any body put knife on her, so doctor treated her with injections and medicine. After a long while they said the 'growth' melted.

About a year after that people noticed that Miss Eslyn belly started swelling up again, but this time it was a different story. It started showing about four months after Mr Touse went back to Tobago. He used to be the overseer on the big estate. For years he went overseas and never came back, as if he turned his back on Grenada. Apparently after their parents died the brothers had a bad quarrel, so Mr Touse packed his grip and went away. He only came back this once, looking meagre and sick. When people travel and come back they usually look nice and fresh but Mammy say she heard when this man came he looked like a spirit. He was supposed to spend six months but after about five weeks he went back. That was just after the night some boys saw him leaving Miss Eslyn house foreday morning with his pants in his hand. When the news broke out, Miss Eslyn threatened to bring people to court if she heard them calling her name. She on again about how she was a good Christian woman, she don't mix up in any nastiness. Then when her belly started swelling again she started hiding from people. This time when the baby was ready to born, by the time they called the nurse, both mother and baby was dead. Miss O'Brien was there looking after the mother when all that happened because she was the oldest girl. Mammy said that she hear that after the mother died Miss O'Brien started making funny noises, just like when the mother was in pain. That's why even now they say she catch mama malady from her mother.

The same kind of noise people said they heard the older woman making long after she died. They say the first time they heard it was the week before carnival, the year the woman died. Mr Nedd first heard her. The story was at first he thought was a baby crying behind Miss Eslyn house, but because it was around carnival time he thought that was somebody practising so he took no notice. Then Miss Luzet talked about a strange noise she heard foreday morning around the same place, only this time it wasn't a child but like a woman moaning. I don't know.

These things happened so long ago people don't remember how it really happened. Sometimes I say to myself these things are not true, but then again, look at Miss O'Brien, look at the macaquee she making with herself. Sometime when Mammy telling me these things, she make it sound as if she was born at that time. Lawd if she was that would make my mother old as Miss O'Brien or Mr Ivor. Mr Ivor, I sure he is the oldest man in the whole parish, if not the whole of Grenada. He so old he really look like a spirit. I know it not nice to say, but I really 'fraid the man. I mean he looked like a dead person walking. One day when I had about 11 I was going up Mt. Plaisir to meet Mammy. As soon as I turn the corner by the golden apple tree under Kakaul by Uncle Cally house, who I boot up on but Mr Ivor. Boop boop, my heart started beating. Boop a toop boop it went, as if it ready to jump out if I open my mouth. I tell you, I turn around and I run. It may sound funny but I thought was a spirit under the tree. To make things worse he saw me running and he was calling me. Who? Me? You must be joking. He met Mammy a little higher up and told how he called me to give me a mango and I run. Mammy wasn't vex with me because she know I was afraid of the old man.

Anyway about that funny noise. Mr Nedd heard it, then foreday morning Miss Luzet heard it. Miss Luzet said it was as if a woman was in pain . . . groaning . . . wailing, groaning, and then the child started crying. The noise was right below Miss Eslyn window. At first people started saying it was a man called Pamsue that was up to his stupidness to frighten people. Others said it was him, but was because morning catch him and he did not have time to change from his lougarou 'self' and the noise was to frighten people away from where he was hiding. Those bad boys in the village started teasing him, making song on him. The more the man say he had nothing to do with anything, the more they teased him. One day a man from Marigot playing brass and square up in Pamsue face and tell him a fuss he make lougarou he don't even know when day light. Pamsue grab his cutlass and plaw, plaw, plapp, he planass the man. Mammy say she heard was one fight in the foreroad that day. Pamsue nearly half kill the man. All the while they teasing Pamsue the police heard them but didn't do anything; as soon as they see Pamsue half killing the man, they locked him. The night he in the police cell the woman and child cried and cried from midnight up to foreday morning. The woman screaming as if she in pain and the child whining as if it hungry.

Another night a man called Evans was going home. They say he used to sleep at a woman over the river, so it was after midnight when he was going to his house. He had to pass behind Miss Eslyn house to go to his. As he reached a boli tree in front her door, he felt sort of funny. His head felt as if it's grown. His tongue filled up his mouth and he started sweating hot and cold and shaking as if he had ague fever. He had an old pan in his hand that he used to bring provision for the woman. His hands became clammy clammy that he could not even hold on to the pan. When he lifted his head and looked under the window he saw a woman sitting on the big stone with a white bundle in her lap. She was rocking backwards and forward and groaning. The man let out one amount of bad word and the woman just vanished. People heard the noise for a long time. They said it's because the woman died in childbirth, that's why she turn mama malady. Her family made a big prayer for her. They said to help her soul rest in peace. Nothing change you know. The same way they made prayer for Miss Sagoo when she drowned saying to help her soul to rest in peace.

Listening to Mammy with these stories, I think to myself she must have a deep hole in her head as well storing up all these things. The best time she used to tell stories is when we sitting down on the step in the evenings. I remember once she was telling me about something that happened when she was small. I couldn't believe things like that could happen. I must of looked at her in a strange way.

'Flora,' she said. 'Chile what I telling you is true. I never see anything like that in my life.'

'Really! What you mean Mammy?'

'Aye aye girl. That was something. I was taking scholarship lessons in Gouyave at the time. I had to work very hard because it was the second chance I had to sit the Government scholarship. I didn't want to take it a third time.'

'Scholarship, Mammy?!' I didn't know you was bright to sit scholarship.' I was only teasing Mammy because people always saying how although I bright I still not as bright as

Mammy was when she was a little girl. They say she was one of the brightest pupil in the Anglican school. How the headmaster always used to praise her. He used to say to the town children how they should be ashamed of themselves, because they used to call the children from the villages country bookie but they had more brains than town children.

'Chupes! What you saying girl? How you mean you didn't know?!'

'Sorry, Mammy. I only joking.'

'Aye aye. The day in question lessons finished early, but I stayed behind liming with my friend.'

'Eh em.' I cleared my throat.

Mammy looked at me under the skin of her eyes. I know there was something else but she was not going to tell me.

'Well,' she went on. 'We limed about on the Lance all evening. I was not thinking about time until my friend noticed that the sun was sinking. With that I decided to put foot in hand and make it down, hoping to meet somebody on Douglastone Bridge going down, or even people coming up from Palmiste.'

Mammy didn't usually tell me about when she was at school, so when she says anything it's like a lesson to me. She used to tell me about how things used to be on the island or in the village; how things changed. Even stories that her mother told her, but not a lot about her own school days, especially after she left government school to go to the church school. If I asked her she'd get vex. Once she talked about a boy who was in her class at school. She only talked about it because Sheila said her mother told her something about when she and Mammy was at school with that person. Sheila did not tell me the whole story, so I asked Mammy what it was about. She started talking about this person, then all of

77

a sudden she started shouting at me, asking me who told me about that. When I told her was something Sheila said her mother told her. Was then she started quarrelling, saying how the woman too damn farse. She should mind her own sallay business instead of minding other people business, especially when thing happens years ago. If I knew she was going to be vex I would of kept my mouth shut. From that day I careful not to mention anything like that again, so when she mentioned about taking scholarship lessons I was eager to hear.

'Was about six o'clock by the time my friend walked with me to Douglastone Bridge and it was already getting dark,' she continued. 'Was the same time that people was saying they seeing Joe Baker sitting down out the cemetery gate with his dog.'

'Joe Baker?' I butted in. 'Who is Joe Baker?'

'Mr Joe. He was a little old man who used to haul gravel by the park. If he not hauling gravel he'd follow the net. He was very friendly. When we going to school he always made little joke with us. After he died people started saying they see him sitting in front the cemetery gate or sometimes on the wall by the boat, he and his dog. Kenneth so coward because he heard the story he wouldn't even walk with me further than the bridge, especially as he had to walk back alone.'

When Mammy said 'Kenneth,' I sort shake, the same time turned and looked at her face. All the while she talking about friend I thinking was a girl. What Sheila said her mother told her flashed through my mind. Anyway I kept my mouth shut, because I wanted to hear more.

'There was not one living soul in sight when we reached the bridge,' she went on. 'I made up my mind to put foot down for the three miles. I left most of my books in the school, so my bag was a bit light. I took out my plimsole and girl I decided to motor. Crickety, crickety crick, cricket started singing. Swick swickety wicket, prickety prickety, lizards started going to bed. I running. Nothing in the road. Not a soul. As I passed the grapefruit tree, just before I reached the dip in the road I heard a strange sound . . . swatch switch swaptch, like donkey having dance on dry leaves. I glanced in the bush . . . nothing. I kept on running. When I turned the corner below Mango Palmer I saw her. Not her, more 'it'. This thing was koublay in the middle of the road. Twist up, twist up like a bundle of old rags. All hair on my body raised up. My toes started sweating. My tongue like a sprinkle it with soda. I looked at this thing in the middle of the road to see if it was going to move. Nothing. Just twisted up.'

Mammy stopped talking as if she taking breath and swallowing her spit. She telling me things that happened years ago, but I tell you I started shaking. Sweat started trickling down my back. My hands became clammy clammy. I didn't realise that I had moved closer to Mammy until I felt her arm around my shoulder and she laughing.

'Flora what do you? How you come near near me so?'

'Lawd, Mammy what you do? You wasn't 'fraid? If was me . . . if was me . . . I don't know. You saying that reminded me about the time you said you got up in the morning with a big round purple mark on your arm.'

'Aaye, I didn't know you remember that. That is different though . . . different altogether. This thing was in the road . . . I getting closer my eyes stick on it. I decided to put myself in the bush as far as possible and keep on running. I took one deep breath and ready to dash. Saye saye the thing was planning too. I ready to dash . . . it ready to move. No head, no legs, it just sort of rolled over right where I was about to pass. Well I wasn't waiting to see anything more. I turned around and Gouyave here I come. I don't know if this thing was behind me or not, I just ran and ran. Ran down the dip, past the grapefruit trees, pass the pougatae vine. As I break the corner towards the bridge in the dusk, I saw somebody coming down. I don't remember if I was glad or more afraid.'

Lawd, Mammy must of been very brave. If was me I don't think I would of been able to move. Mammy talking and the same time I want to pee, but I couldn't go to the latrine – not by myself. I glanced round the corner of the house. The shadows of the leaves of the golden apple trees were like when the Pentecostal people dancing with the spirit in them. I wasn't going there on own. I felt my panty wet a little bit. I squeezed my legs together.

'Bonjay Mammy, suppose was the thing that kind of jumped ahead of you and now pretending to be somebody.'

'Aaye. I didn't think of that. I kept running. As we got closer, I saw was Mr Scott who was living in the old house in LaPoutree. I tell you I was glad. He was a friendly old man who always looked out for us when we going to school. By the time I reached him I was shaking like I had ague fever.'

"What's the matter chile? Eh, what do you?" he asked.

"Down dey, down dey so," I stammered, "down dey . . . by . . . by de mango tree."

"By de mango tree!" I felt his eyes kind of light up. "I saw you going down. I thought you a bit late, but when I saw your friend with you I say you will be alright. Then I saw him going back. These young men . . . I don't

80

know . . . I don't know." He shook his head. He didn't say it bad or anything, like some other big people would do. "Come on," he continued, "doh worry, nothing will trouble you. You said by the mango tree. You mean the Mango Palmer!"

I shook my head. "Yeh somethin in the road roll up."

"Roll up in the road under the mango tree." He said it as if he wanted to be sure of what he heard me say.

"Yeh in the middle of the road. The thing kind of double up double up."

"You sure is not that stupid woman in Boawden making pappyshow with she self?"

"You mean Miss O'Brien?" I answered.

"Yeh, she. She always making stupidness to frighten people."

"Is not her," I said. "I know the lady. People always saying she making tricks but I never see her, but I'm sure it's not her. I'm sure some of the things they say is nancy story."

Mr Scott gave me one of those you-young-people-don't-know-nothing look. "Come on. Let's go," he said. For an old man he could walk fast. I had to do a little run to keep with him.'

'But Mammy you didn't feel more 'fraid?' I butted in. 'I know you said you knew Mr Scott, but it was late and just you, him and that thing in this dangerous place.' The pee was really coming down by that time. Very quietly I said, 'Mammy, Mammy come in the latrine with me. I want to pee.'

Mammy burst out laughing. Really laughing. 'Girl you real coward, you know. Look how long this thing happen.

Long before you born. Mr Scott dead and gone a long long time – you telling me you 'fraid until you pee youself?!'

Mammy came with me to the latrine. Quick quick I finished peeing. My panty was wet but I wasn't going inside to change it to come back outside. 'What happened?' I asked. 'Was the thing still there when you and Mr Scott reached under the mango tree?' I was very curious.

'It was there alright. Heh, as we turned the corner the thing just rolled on one side of the road. I turned around ready to do another sprint, but Mr Scott grabbed me. "Come on," he said. "Come on." With that he started cursing bad word. Was as if he had forgotten that I was with him, because he turned to me and said "Sorry". His cutlass was gripped tight tight in his hand, as if ready to chop up whatever in the road. All of a sudden I started breaking wind . . . purp, prup, prup, purp. I tried to squeeze it back but fright was more than me . . . pruuup, prup, purp, the wind came out. I grabbed Mr Scott shirt tail as if my life depended on it. We going towards this thing, Mr Scott cutlass in his hand, me breaking wind like a car backfiring. Then the thing started unfolding. In the dusk I couldn't make out which part of the body, then I make out her head. How she was folded, nobody could of seen her head, foot or anything, just something roll up like a bundle of old rags. It seemed like her head was between her foot, the foot curved round her bam. Don't ask me where her hands were. When she heard Mr Scott cursing and threatening she untwisted herself and sat down in the grass by the road with some old rags on her lap as if she waiting for something. Mr Scott said it was Miss O'Brien, but I'm not sure because I didn't look at her face and it was dark anyway. From that day, though, I didn't trust her.'

'Bonjay Mammy, it look as if Miss O'Brien making jumbie since she born,' I said.

'Chupes,' Mammy said. 'This woman born old. Sometimes I'm sure she and her mother is one. Since I small the woman old old, and the things your grandmother used to tell me about Miss O'Brien mother is exactly the things the woman doing. Sometimes it's like the dead woman living in the one who is alive.'

I laughed. Mammy used to say some really funny things . . . you ever hear dead people could live in somebody who is alive?! The way Mammy talk you would think she is an old person, but she only have about 30 something, or even just 40. Nobody could look at my mother and say she is old. Her face always fresh and bright. Not a line in her face. When she dress up to go to church or a party or something she look like a twenty-year-old, just like my big sister. Anyway people always say Grenada women don't show their age. Some people you could look in their face and tell how much years they have, but it not easy with Grenada women. Is true, because not only Mammy. Look at Miss Chrissie, I am sure she older than Mammy, but her face fresh and nice. Sometimes me and Mammy going good good. Sometimes again she get vex for nothing. That does make me think perhaps it's like that when you get a little older. If I ask her a little question she would tell me not to ask her stupidness. There are some things that people do that are very strange. Strange but I am still curious to find out why they do them and if there are any meaning behind them. For instance, when somebody died, the bed they slept must be turned around, and if there is bucket of water in the room when the person died the water must be thrown out. The older people say these customs came from Africa during slavery. When I

83

ask Mammy if she knows anything about why they did these things she says since she small people doing these things, and they always have different reason.

Some of it is true, it really come from Africa. Other times she would say people too damn stupid, when they don't have anything to do they sit down by the road, drink white rum and talk rubbish. Perhaps some is old rum talk but I am sure there are something in what they say about the African customs. Another thing is, I suppose, with people like Miss O'Brien making pappyshow all their lives, when they die the stories around their lives stay behind and become some kind of legend. This Miss O'Brien is really something. The way I took my two eyes and see her standing on the sea stone that day, since I born I never see anything like that. This old old woman you know, standing on big stone in the middle of the sea. I don't know. Sheila gone now. I sure she would be surprise to see the old lady still alive.

The day the slipper burst was a good thing Sheila was with me because I don't know what I would of done. Mammy preached to me that I must be careful with things, especially when somebody give it to me. Although I didn't burst it by spite I know Mammy wouldn't believe me. She would say is drag; I dragged my foot. When Miss Eva boy wasn't there to fix the strap I was a bit upset. Sheila took a lace from her crêpe sole and tied it up for me until we reached Mr Morgan in Marigot. Was really Sheila he fixed it for, because he and her mother was good friend.

5

Me and Sheila was friends since we very small.
Mammy didn't mind us going to each other's house, but
there were some children she didn't let me play with. Like
the Whiteman children who lived in the gap by the old road
on the other side of the ravine. These children rude rude.
Always cursing and fighting. I don't know who worse, them
or Miss Bayne children. The same way those mothers don't
have any reasoning for their children. One day Mr Nedd left
his pan by the road for the kerosene man to full up. He
folded the money and put it under the pan. Miss Whiteman
two older boys took the man money, wrap stone in the paper
and full the pan of water.. Was a good thing Miss Emily saw
them and told Mr Nedd, otherwise when the man think is
kerosene he putting in his lamp it would of been water – and
the whole thing could of blow up in his face. When Mr Nedd
went and complain, exactly what Miss Bayne did when Mr
George went to her, the same thing Miss Whiteman did.
You wouldn't think that there would be two mothers the
same would you! Instead of chastising the children, she called
them inside and pretending to beat them while they bawling
blue murder. She not satisfied with trying to fool Mr Nedd;
she then went in Miss Emily yard and cursed her, calling her

mama malady child and telling her how she looked like lajabless. She knew her children wrong, but she said the woman should shut her mouth. Is all that why Mammy don't let me play with any of the children. She said she don't have time to beat taebay with anybody. When people ignorant is ignorant they ignorant. They could read book but still blind like bat.

They say is confusion Miss Whiteman making, that's why her husband left she and the children. He said he can't stay with that kind of woman. He spent a lot of money to build a nice comfortable house for his family, but the wife so miserable and worthless he couldn't stand it. In the end he took up with a woman in LaBaye. I don't know if was true. Was Sheila who used to tell me things that happened in the village. She said Mr Whiteman spent years in Aruba. He used to send plenty of money for his wife to look after her and the children to build a decent house. When he came home looking for house, the state the place in he felt so shame. Was a good thing he came with some money. Quick quick he managed to build a decent place. When he asked his wife about the money he sent home, the woman started one bacanal in the place, saying he never sent any money and anyhow the children growing big and things for them expensive. Mr Whiteman wouldn't of minded if that was true. But the only good things the children had was what he posted to them. Miss Whiteman couldn't show him anything she bought over the years. Everybody knew where the money went. The woman so stupid her husband working hard in another country and sending money for her to look after, it she taking it and bring give Dillon to work obeah. Dillon had the right idea, although it almost cost him his life. If people have money to throw way, he might as well

86

take it from them. He lived up the road to Concorde mountain. The right place to practise his nastiness. When people going home late in the evening he would make funny funny noise like evil spirits having convention to frighten people and animals.

One evening about six o'clock Peter, Miss Redhead grandson, was going home. When he reached below the golden apple tree in Dillon gap his dog started whining and wouldn't go any further. All call Peter, calling the dog it won't budge. It just won't pass Dillon house. It was whining and prancing backward. Peter could not see anything, but he too became very frightened. Although he could not see anything, the smell around the house was something else. It was sickening. It was like all old bush burning together with Jeyes and cacajab sprinkled over it. Peter said he grabbed the dog by the neck and ran until he reached Two Rock. That's how Dillon used to fool people. Burn old nastiness around his house, rub with the ashes and walk about with beard like black rice grain covering his face, making people think he was the biggest obeah man in the place. The truth was he couldn't even boil a good cup of bush tea. People don't listen when he speak, they say he say stupidness when he drink the rum, but was the truth he was telling them. He always said if people stupid and don't have use for their money he would take it from them. That's how he managed to eat Mr Whiteman money he worked so hard for in Aruba. People said Miss Whiteman used to gamble in the bay with the fishermen. Gamble and drink out all the money. When Mr Whiteman send and say he coming home, she went to Dillon to work obeah to make her husband stay in Aruba. Apparently she had to put something in a letter and post to Mr Whiteman; obviously that didn't work because the man came home. After he build the house and everything, he heard what happened to his money. He went to Dillon house and beat him up. I hear if it wasn't for people going to the garden and heard Dillon bawling, Mr Whiteman would of killed him. I never see anything like that. After the bacanal the man packed his things and went to live with the La Baye woman. There was a lot more, but I didn't understand it.

Sheila used to tell me things, but just after that happened she and her family moved away. I missed her very much. Even though she went and mixed with that crooked priest, we still remained friends. In some ways I didn't understand her mother. The girl joined the Anglican church because she wanted to make first communion and then confirm; when she said she going back to the Catholic church her mother should make stay where she was. She knew Sheila had too much thing in her skin so she should make her stay in the Anglican church. After the scandal in the church, and things settled down with a new priest coming and thing, what you think Sheila did?! Instead of either staying there and taking her vows, or even coming back to the Anglican church, she kept following all kind of preacher that come and preach in the foreroad. Just before they moved away she joined the Holy Fire of Christ church down by Brizan.

I don't know where this one came from. Everyday a new religion start up in the place. Mammy said the man that said he was the pastor in that Holy Fire of Christ church was nothing more than a damn thief. She said he used to work on Palmiste estate and they catch him thiefing the estate nutmeg. Well not catch him to lock him up. He got away because he stowaway to Trinidad on the trafficking boat. The overseer on the estate set a trap to catch him; by the time he went to McDowell house, the bag of marked nutmeg was there but he disappeared. Months later a woman came home and said she saw him in Port of Spain. She said when they came to face face he couldn't look in her eye ah fuss he shame. Although the woman was not in Grenada when the scandal broke out, everybody knows you don't need radio in Grenada. With people trafficking between the islands – and anyway half of Trinidad people have family in Grenada – news travel faster than African drums. The woman said she just said 'Howdy', like she don't know anything, but you could of seen how he started sweating, wiping his face with a piece of dirty kerchief. She said the way he dabbed his face brow, scleup, it was clear he was under some kind of pressure. That's the last anybody heard of him for a long time. His little house under the rock stayed empty for a long time, until his sister son moved in with his friend.

Years later, perhaps about five, I don't remember exactly, McDowell decided to come home. He came with a heavy bible, saying he'd seen the light. From then every Sunday morning, pling pling, bell bawling in the foreroad while McDowell hollowing out saying he spreading the word of God. People so stupid, they never learn. As soon as anyone come with a bible they forget the teaching of their church and follow them. Anyway, people started saying how McDowell is a changed man . . . he has seen the light. Next thing he have a whole load of people behind him. The man come from Trinidad with a bible and an old grip, two twos he buy a big new car and started living life. After a few weeks preaching in the foreroad he moved to the big society hall. People going to his meeting, giving him money and things. He hardly had to buy food with his money. Every little thing the people gave him, saying he see the light in truth. They bringing their things, he telling them to give generously, their reward would be great in heaven. All the while the man is the biggest burburl man in the place, taking the people money and building big house in Paradise. Not even in Brizan where he first had his base, but way up in Paradise. What people did not know was that he had to run away from Trinidad. The authority got news of what he was doing and was after him.

When Sheila gone I thought she went oversea with her mother. Next thing I hear she up in Paradise living in McDowell house. I don't know what does happen to some people in their head. I missed her, though. When they moved away, one of her cousins moved into the house. With the woman there looking after the place everything looked alright. The place was nice and clean, then after about eighteen months she left and gone to America. Within a few weeks around the house looked like nobody ever lived there for years. Like the front yard never seen a cutlass. It was a shame to see the flower garden looking like a wilderness. When Mammy came and say she see people moving in there, I was glad in one way and not too glad at the same time. I was hoping they would be clean people. People who would look after the place. Although we lived a little way from the house, still it's nice when everywhere around is clean. Another thing I was wondering if they were friendly people. I felt better when I saw a girl sitting on the step one evening and a woman in the kitchen window. I could not see her clearly but she looked a bit younger than me. I said evening to the woman, she looked friendly, but I didn't speak to the girl.

The first time I saw them was the Tuesday evening. By Saturday they had new curtain up in the living room. I noticed a woman, a little girl, and sometimes a man is with them. I never saw him close, but even from far he looked just like the man Nenen Beatrice was telling Mammy about the other day when she passed by us. She was trying to make Mammy remember the man, because it looked as if he belonged to Grand Roy but went away for some years. Nenen Beatrice was telling Mammy that that Mr Ben came home with a woman saying is his wife. The thing was Mr Ben met this woman in Petit Martinique, but she really from Venezuela. They take up with one another and she followed him to Grenada, saying she is Mrs Ben. Nenen Beatrice talking to Mammy and I outside playing I washing the two piece of clothes in the basin. Funny how things work out sometimes. It was like this: Mr Ben was friendly with a woman in the village. Then she met somebody she knew before and she didn't want Mr Ben any more, so he left the island. After a couple of years he come back with this other woman. Well what a confusion! What happen is the first woman is now on her own with her little girl and Mr Ben still liked her. It turned out that the woman he came with was not his 'married' wife. She on and on at him to marry her. He kept on promising and promising, but when he heard that his long-time friend was alone he decided he wanted her, so he told the Venezuela woman he not ready to marry yet. She gave him a piece of cursing down. Tell him she not living in sin anymore. If he don't want to marry her how she leaving him. Well that's just what he wanted; as she packed her bag and went back to Petit Martinique he started visiting his old friend.

The man is the same person Nenen Beatrice was talking about, by the way she described him. One evening I was coming from school and the girl was on the step playing with the flower pan. For a minute she looked just like my sister Janice. Same way how Janice used to turn her fingers between the flowers to pick out the dead leaves, same way the girl did. I stood looking at her with my mouth opened. It's six years since Janice died but I still miss her very much. A long time after she died I used to run in the house calling her. In the night was the worse time. We used to sleep together in one bed. Sometimes we would fight to sleep in front away from under the window. We were afraid that evil spirits would come through the window at night, especially after the morning Miss Mabel woke up saying lougarou suck her the night before. She had a big round red mark on her leg. They said it's the pipe mark . . . the lougarou mark. From that last thing Miss Mabel does at night was to put a pair of shoes upside down in front the door. From the minute me and Janice heard that, we were more afraid. We pulled the bed way from under the window but we still fight in the night to sleep in front.

One night, about midnight, I heard something moving about in front the door. It sounded like somebody was moving things about. I crept into Mammy's room quiet quiet to wake her up, but she already heard it. She got up, took the cutlass from behind the door, went to the hall and listened. We listened for a few minutes. Was as if whoever was there was rearranging the flower tins on the step. That went on for a few minutes then everything stopped. Janice was the sort of person who even they fast asleep breeze blow it would wake them up, but she said she did not hear anything. She said she did not hear anything, not even when I got out of bed, but yet what she did when she got up? Even before we asked her anything? The first thing she did was go outside and started straightening the flowers on the step. The way she did that as if she knew somebody had interfered with them. And the look on her face . . . it was so sad. Sad as if she lost something. Mammy asked her what was wrong. All she said was 'Nothing'. Just so: 'Nothing'. Mammy looked at her and was as if there was water in her eyes. I felt sort of funny. I can't explain it . . . just funny.

Mammy said she knew something was not right. Not exactly wrong, but not right either. She said she had that funny feelings running through her body. As if she was two persons . . . herself and someone inside her waiting . . . waiting for something to happen. It was Saturday and we were home doing the housework as usual. All day Mammy only looking at Janice . . . just looking at her and shaking her head. The girl wasn't sick but she was different. Me and her usually go to do the shopping for Mammy. Normally Janice don't even want to carry the towel with the bread, saying she too little to carry it, but that day she wanted to carry the basket. We suppose to sweep around the house together. Apart from cleaning her flowers she never wanted to touch a broom. I had to quarrel with her to help do anything. That day she could not find enough to do. Before Mammy do . . . Janice was ready. All the while singing . . . singing hymns. Singing all the Sunday school songs. At the time it didn't bother me, but thinking about now makes my blood run cold. Mammy was very worried. I heard her telling Mr Mano how Janice acting strange and she felt as if there was some sort of spirit around the child. By the next Saturday my sister was dead . . . dead . . . dead. Just eight days later and Janice was gone.

Now, six years later, I still don't understand it. Mammy on about it is God's work. He knows best. Me, I don't understand why he had to take my sister. She only had 5. Never did anything to anybody. I don't understand what sin she could have committed for God to take her. She was a bit forward for her age, but still she didn't hurt anybody. She used to make people laugh with the things she used to say. One day after Catechism lessons I asked Cannon Johnson why God had to take my sister. He said the same thing as Mammy . . . God knows best.

All during that week Janice was alright and not alright, if you know what I mean. She spent a lot of time under the big hibiscus tree under Mammy window. Friday we came from school everything was alright. When Mammy ready to cook dinner Janice asked her to cook some macaroni for her. I was surprised because she knew what we usually eat on Friday nights. Sometimes on Saturday we would have macaroni with beef and little little dumplings but that's when Mammy give us castor oil to wash out. Janice knew that, so it was funny that she should ask Mammy for macaroni Friday night. Mammy told her she was stewing some jacks for dinner.

'I don't want any jacks. I want some macaroni,' Janice demanded. 'I see you buy cow meat; I want piece with some macaroni.'

'The meat is for dinner on Sunday,' Mammy reminded her.

'I want some macaroni. I don't want any jacks,' she emphasised. I looked at her, then at Mammy, thinking she asking for a beating. We always eat whatever Mammy cooked, not say what we want to eat . . . Well, perhaps sometimes. But it was the way Janice was demanding the macaroni. Before Mammy said or did anything, the girl left where she was on the step and came in the kitchen. Stood right in front of Mammy. Her eyes fixed straight in Mammy face and she was shaking like a leaf.

'Janice, Janice what do you? You sick. What's the matter?'

When I heard the anxiety in Mammy voice, I joined them in the kitchen. Janice turned, looked at me, then back at Mammy, and went outside under the hibiscus tree.

'What do Janice?' I asked. 'How she shaking so?'

'I don't know,' Mammy mumbled. Deep lines appeared across her forehead. She rubbed her hand across her face. 'I don't know,' she repeated more to herself. I knew she was very worried. It was so unusual for Janice to act that way. Not only asking for the food but the way she was shaking. I felt a bit scared as well. Anyway, Mammy took the meat and started cutting up to cook instead of the jacks. I peeped to see what Janice was doing. She was sitting on the stone by the hibiscus tree. Just sitting there with her hands in her lap. After a few minutes, Mammy said she going by cousin Joey for a piece of yam to put with the dumpling. It was about five o'clock. Normally on Fridays after school we don't have any housework to do, because on Saturday morning we give the place a good clean . . . wash, scrub, sweep everything, everywhere from top to bottom. With nothing to do, Janice is usually either with her story book she borrow from the library or next door with her friend Karen, but today she is sitting under the tree. I sat on the step in front door thinking. All of a sudden I heard a sniffing. When I listened I realised it was Janice crying. I got up to go to her, but before I covered the few steps I heard her speaking to someone. 'No, leave me alone,' she was saying. 'I don't want to come with you.' She went talking to whoever it was, telling them to leave her alone. She don't want to leave me and Mammy.

'Jan,' I called her. 'Janice!' I stood in front her, my hand on her shoulder. 'Janice,' I spoke to her again. She did not seem to know I was there. She went on talking. Tears streaming down her face. When I looked on the ground in front her I noticed she had vomited. The vomit was yellow like buttercup. There were chunks of white things in it. I tell you . . . fright took hold of me. I took her hand to bring her inside. 'Come,' I said. 'Come inside.' Janice could not move. She was stiff as a wall. 'Come inside Janice,' I coaxed her. She stook rigid, looking at the vomit. Her face streaked with eye water, her eyes glassy like marble. That was enough. I belted down the road towards cousin Joey shouting for Mammy. As she heard me bawling, Mammy rushed from cousin Joey. As soon as I told her about the vomit she started bawling. Cousin Joey called cousin Melda and they started running towards our house. When we reached home Janice was stretched out under the hibiscus tree . . . stretched out as if she dead. Cousin Melda helped Mammy bring her in the house, while cousin Joey rushed round to Calib to get his car to bring Janice to the hospital in town. All the time everybody running with this and that to rub Janice, I bawling. They rubbed her with bayrum, cacajab all kind of things, still, nothing; she laid on the bed stiff. Three o'clock me and my sister came from school good good. It's not even six o'clock and she gone all funny as if she dead already. Since the night we heard whatever was outside shifting the flower pans Janice was not the same. I thought of all that happened during that week. Mammy was thinking about it as well. I heard her telling cousin Melda about it. Cousin Melda tell her she should of bathe Janice with holy water and sprinkled some around the house. They said a lot of things which I did not understand at the time. Even six years I still don't understand some of them. I suppose some of them are customs that came from Africa as well, perhaps not sprinkling holy water but something like that.

They rushed Janice to the hospital. I stayed behind because

the car was not big enough to hold me. Cousin Melda and cousin Joey wife went with Mammy. She said Janice opened her eyes only once. She looked in Mammy eyes but it was as if she was looking at a stranger. She laid in Mammy arms, all talk, they talked to her . . . nothing. Was as if she was in another world. Mammy said she was so frightened she wanted to prayer, but she could not remember any prayers. She said, to make matters worse, when they reached the hospital the doctor who examined her the child started shouting at her. He got vex. He shouted telling her she waited until the child is almost dead before she brought her to him. He said it might be too late to save the child, and if the worse happened he would consider reporting Mammy to the police for starving the child. When Mammy told cousin Melda what the doctor said, I hear cousin Melda marched into the room where he was with the sick child and gave him a good piece of her mind. She tell him if anybody wanted food is him, and he better get on and do his job properly otherwise she would be doing the reporting. All the time Mammy telling him what happened earlier he wasn't listening. Because Janice was thin, that's the way she always was, and because of the sickness her face became dusky pale, before he examine the child properly to started saying she suffering from malnutrition. When Mammy told us the story she said when cousin Melda finished with the doctor his colour changed. Quick quick he got another doctor to examine the child. Was then they found out that she contracted some kind of virus. I didn't understand then, and even now I still don't understand. All I know is my sister never came back to sleep with me.

The night she was in the hospital Mammy and cousin Melda stayed in town with one of Mammy friend to be nearby if anything should happen. Tanty Clarice, my grandmother and some cousins came to stay with me. Plenty people came to the house that night. Some just pass to say they sorry to hear Janice was sick. Some stay a little while to keep us company. Miss Chrissie and her husband stayed almost all night. Miss Peter came with her bible and said some prayers. She said if Janice don't get better, it's God's work. I couldn't accept that. I don't understand why the same God we prayer to for peace and all things that was good should make a little child sick and perhaps die.

Next morning me and Tanty Clarice went down to the hospital on the first bus. When we got there, Mammy and cousin Melda and the other woman was already there. The doctor had just taken Mammy to the room where Janice was. Me, cousin Melda, Tanty Clarice and Mammy friend sat on a bench in the corridor.

We sat there saying nothing, just staring at the door where Mammy and the doctor went. Everything was sort of quiet. Then like a sharp thunder break, one scream pierced the silence. Just one screech. It sounded like when an owl screech over a house when someone is going to die. Cousin Melda and Miss Agnes moved to stand in front the door. It was only one scream but we knew it was Mammy. After that everything went quiet. Not a sound. It was like the birds closed their beaks. Like the sea behind the hospital stopped the waves from dashing on the shore. Like the whole world stopped. I sat on the bench like a statue. I wanted to get up. Wanted to push everybody aside and rush in that room to Mammy and Janice, but I could not move. I tried to stand up but my feet felt like all the bones had gone, there was nothing to hold up my body. I could not even bawl out, my mouth would not open. My heart and temples were having competition to see which one would out-thump-thumpity-thump each other. I felt my chest heaving, my head pumping, my eyes bulging, yet I could not react. The doctor came through the door holding up who I thought of first to be an old woman. The woman's hands were sort of holding her head in place while the doctor holding up her body. Before the doctor turned towards us, cousin Melda was by his side embracing Mammy. Miss Agnes bellowed out one 'Lawd have mercy, have mercy, have mercy'. Me, to this day, I can't remember how or when I moved from my fixture. Whatever it was holding me back let loose, I was picked up and thrown into Mammy's arms. I hang on to my her, just bawling, bawling.

She didn't recognise any of us around her. With her hands bracing her head, she was shaking as if she had spasm and making funny grunting noise. She didn't look like my mother at all. She looked weak and helpless.

Although I had five years more than her, Janice was more womanish than me. I really missed her. She used to say things as if she was a big woman. One day I heard cousin Melda telling Mammy Janice too big for her age. She didn't come to stay long. She said things like Janice is an old head on a young body, and she only come to tease us. Mammy laughed. There are other things people said about Janice that I never thought about at the time but since she died I can't help thinking about them. Janice used to ask question that I wouldn't think about asking. Like the day she asked Mammy where our father was. Mammy was vex, real vexed. There were times I wanted to ask Mammy for him, but after what Mammy once said I kept my mouth shut, but not Janice. The day she kept questioning Mammy about our father, Mammy shouted at her. 'You is a Williams,' she said. 'Janice

Williams, and you father in St. Croix. Don't ask me no question. Don't let me hear you with any more stupidness.'

Janice was not satisfied. She said she never seen our father. Nobody had ever seen him. If he really in St. Croix, why don't he come to Grenada to see us? She went on and on that evening. In the end, Mammy gave her one box across her face that shut her up. Mammy said Janice go on as if she had some kind of jumbie on her. I didn't understand why Mammy got so angry, but for some reason she did not want to hear my father name mention. She said if he wanted to stay in St. Croix and make macaquee with himself she don't want to have anything to do with him. I think there was more. Is something to do with the time she went to St. Croix to meet him. Before that a man from Grenville brought a letter for Mammy from my father. After that, now and again we used to get a letter from him with a little money in it. One day he sent quite a bit of money, telling Mammy to come and meet him. He said she could come for three months or so and if she likes it she would come back for us, that was me and my brother Christopher at the time. At first Mammy said she not going anyway. If he wanted to see the family, why don't he come home, unless he threw stone behind his back when he left Grenada. Cousin Melda and some others coaxed her, coaxed her. They told her she should go and see what he doing. In the end Mammy decided to go, leaving me and my brother with my grandmother. She said if she don't like what she see, she would be back before first cock crow. Well we know Mammy, but although we missed her we did not expect her back within the month. She said if she don't like what she saw she coming back. Well that was 13 June; by the end of June she was back home. All she said was that the man she married turn veaneage, and she not

100

joining him in any nastiness in other people country. He wrote to us after, but Mammy just tore up the letters. Janice never saw him, could be why she was on and on at Mammy about him. And could be why people said there was something about her that made her so advanced for her age. I don't know. I don't understand.

She died the Saturday morning. Mammy wanted to bury her the same day, but something or the other was not ready so the funeral had to be the Sunday. That Saturday night it rained as if God was emptying all his buckets. The rain fell and so it made hot. They said God sent the rain to make it easier to handle the mould to cover the grave. As the rain pelted down, so the sea bawling like old cow . . . rook a toook, rook a took, splash splash splush. The waves battered the big stones towards Marigot on one side and towards LaPoutree on the other. Miss Chrissie was worried because Janice grave was already dug under the big Christmas tree in the burial ground by the bay. Miss Chrissie was worried in case the waves break away and roll up and full the grave of water. Thank God that did not happen. For a little child I never see so much people at a funeral. They came from all over the island. Family we had not seen for years turned up. Some who knew Janice and her womanishness joked about the things she did. One woman who worked in the nutmeg pool with Mammy said she remembered when me and Janice spent the day with Mammy at her work. How Janice teased the women; how they were cracking the nutmeg . . . crack a crack, clack a clack, clickety click, then the hands running through the nutmeg trays truch . . . scrutch . . . a truchsh sh.

When the actual burial started, although I was bawling I was very worried for Mammy. All our families and lots of friends were bawling. Even my brother Christopher who came over when he heard the news, he was bawling. Everybody was crying, but with Mammy that was something else. I thought she had gone mad. She didn't want anybody to touch the coffin. When time come to put it in the grave, they had to hold her back otherwise she was going in the grave too. I was scared. I could not even sing the hymns for my sister. They sang her favourite hymns. The ones she liked from Sunday school like 'There is a friend for little children, above the bright blue sky', and 'Jesus loves me this I know, for the bible tells me so'. I remember thinking, if Jesus loves us why is Janice dead? Perhaps what the priest said is true that God has a plan for all of us. I don't know. After six years I still don't understand. Some days I don't think of Janice, but then just a little thing would remind of her, like seeing that girl on the step. Same way how Janice used to turn her head and hands, same way the girl doing.

I must of forgotton myself, just staring at the girl, because I did not hear anybody behind me until the person said 'Morning'. The lady, she must be the girl's mother was right behind me.

'Morning,' I said.

'You know Gloria?' she asked.

'No Ma'am, I just watching how she weeding the flowers.'

'O hoye,' she smiled. Her eyes sort of dipped when she smiled. Her top lip covered all her teeth. 'I thought perhaps you meet her in school. We just move her, you know.'

'I know. I was just watching her. The way she bend over the flowers reminded me of my sister before she died.' I don't usually speak to strangers but this lady was sort of nice. Her face was friendly. It just came out about my sister being dead.

102

'Sorry to hear about your sister,' she said. 'I see you passing. You live up the road by the golden apple tree?'

'Yes Ma'am,' I started to walk away.

'How they call you?' she asked.

'Flora, Ma'am,' I said. 'Flora Williams.'

'Gloria,' she called the girl. 'Come and tell Flora howdy. She living in the house you was talking about the other day.'

The woman was friendly, but the girl looked so stuck up. Her mother speak to her, all she did was turn side ways and skin up her mouth as she smell something. I don't know; people brains really funny. The way the girl skinned up her mouth made me think of the first set of people who lived in the house, I mean long before Sheila and her family lived there. This woman and her daughter could be third or even fourth cousins to them, because they have the same red skin and dougla hair.

Mammy said she heard the woman who built the house came from St. Vincent. That must be a long time ago, because Mammy says she didn't even know the old woman but she knew the grandchildren. Apparently the woman used to traffick. Move about from one island to another. Not only selling things but she used to preach as well. I could tell you something; one way to make friends quick quick in Grenada is to pick up a bible. Although she had been to places like Tobago, St. Marteens and Montserrat, she liked Grenada the best. The first time she came to Grenada she liked the place, she started coming regularly and after a while she decided to stay. At first she rented a little house and still selling her things. Even trafficking to the other islands as usual, but instead of going back to St. Vincent she made her home in Grenada. Then she pick up with a man called Moses up in Belvedere. They moved to Grand Roy where he built a little

103

house for them. After about a year they married. The people stopped calling her 'Vincee'; she was just Miss Mo. Mammy say she heard the first house was only two little rooms but they added bit by bit and buy up more of the land around, so by the time they had their six children it was a very big house with about two-and-half acre of land. Another thing; Mammy always says you see today but you don't see tomorrow. People seeing only that little two-bedroom house on the land, now would not believe it was once a 'mansion'. I don't know what happened, perhaps nobody could really remember, could be as the family grew up and moved away the people sold off the land and because they could not afford to repair the house only fixed up two rooms. I don't know but whatever the reason only a small two-room house was there by the time Sheila and her family moved in. I know Sheila since I very small because we used to live near by in the other place. Apart from jumping from one church to the other she and her family was alright. But then you could see somebody everyday and don't really know them. Is when something break out you know who is who. After all the confusion with Miss Sagoo and then the crooked priest, somehow things started to go wrong with them. The sister that they sent away to have Mr Moore baby never came back. Then the brothers went overseas and don't even looked behind them. I think one went to Martinique. I don't know where the other one went. I don't think the boys ever write one line to the family. It sort of funny beause they were always like a happy family.

Mammy always used to say is not all skin teeth is good laugh, and when you digging pit make sure you dig two. Another thing she used to say was: bat turned to mess on God, it mess on itself. That used to make me laugh. I don't

104

know where she used to get these things. When I asked her how bat expected to mess on God, she'd laugh and say 'Eh eh girl! Why you tink bat always flying with its bam in the air?!'

It looked as if Sheila parents used to work nastiness to make the children get on, like pass examinations and get things they wanted. Even with all that, the boys still turned out worthless. The one that went to Martinique, his father wanted him to be a lawyer. The boy dunce as bat. He couldn't even pass School Leaving Examination, much less lawyer exam. But the father wanted him to be lawyer. He got a job with a lawyer in Church Street, St. Georges for the boy, telling him he could start his training from there. All the while was brains he boxing on the son. It was a whole mix up.

Lawd I tell you people brain must be really funny. I would like to see how it works. I mean bringing up all things that happened years and years gone to the front. Just imagine I started remembering all these things while I in church witnessing the two teachers getting married. I suppose if teacher Marion grandmother didn't bawl out, all these things would stay in the bottom on my brain.

Well about this lawyer business, the brango was a man in Grenville used to work obeah for Mr Endly, that's Sheila father. He used to bring all his money to the man, until his money ran out. The Grenville man told him was alright, because he was a good customer he could pay him when he had the money. Long time passed and he still can't pay. So the Grenville man took him to court, saying the money was for doing this that and the other. I laughed when I heard that. I wonder what the magistrate would of said if the man had put on the paper the money was for making obeah.

105

Anyway, Mr Endly go and put town lawyer on the case, but he couldn't pay him either. So he said to the lawyer if he gives his son a job, every month he could take something out of the boy money. Anyway that was settled. Jeremy started working for the lawyer. The first month he looking for money he got nothing. The lawyer gave him some old cock and bull story. When he told his father, he said not to worry, just keep his mind on the work and things would work out. Jeremy was looking forward to learning some legal stuff. Instead the lawyer had him running up and down the island serving papers like a bailiff.

Everyday Mr Endly asking him how he getting on. How much work he did that day and things like that. Not like he was interested in knowing what the boy was learning but as if he had something on his mind. Jeremy was suspicious. One day the lawyer sent him to St. Davids to serve some papers on somebody, the boy mislaid the papers. The lawyer went mad; you would think was a million dollars the boy lost. The lawyer called him all names under the sun. When he cursing him his tongue slipped and he let out how the boy family making obeah and how the father owe him money for defending him against the obeah man in Grenville, that is why he gave the boy the job. How the boy father owe obeah man money and he can't pay him. Jeremy was so vex; he told the lawyer he is an old liar, took up his things and left the job the same time. He was vex and shame as well, especially as there were people in the lawyer office who knew the family. He took the first bus going home. Not even waiting for his regular bus. He expected his father to go and threaten the lawyer for scandalising the family name; instead the man started on him. He started on the usual thing how he worked so hard to send him to school, but then it came

106

out that the money he owed the man in Grenville was for making obeah, and he couldn't pay the lawyer either; that's why he sent Jeremy to work for him.

The boy could not stand it, he could believe that his father was that sort of person. He asked his mother if she knew anything about it, all she did was pammed her lips and looked in the distance as if she did not understand what was happening. From that day Jeremy never spoke to his father again. The next week he packed his things and went overseas. He told his mother he is going away but not a word to his father. The man took it to heart, and on top that he lost the case so now he owed the lawyer and the Grenville man. Things went from bad to worse. He started drinking more than usual. Drinking the old white rum and crying trouble to everybody. He was nearly always drunk, in so much that he lost his job. They cautioned him many times but as if the bottle became his God, in the end they sacked him.

All that time Sheila and her mother going to church as if nothing happening. Sometimes though Sheila would be very quiet . . . just not saying anything. Sometimes as if she in another world. If I ask her anything she would shout at me. Thing burst out about six month after her brother left.

6

One morning early Mr Terry going in the mountain. He said he don't know what made him go the long way instead of cutting across Mr Black cane piece. He said, just as he passed the mango sharray, his mind tell him to across over the little ravine that run alongside the big plum tree. The first thing he noticed was an old felt hat hanging on a branch. When he looked again he saw as if somebody propped up against the tree. Strange he thought; who would be out here so early unless is lougarou that let day light catch it? He whistled his dog, tightened the grip on the cutlass and edged nearer to see better. Slow slow he went up to the person, each step calling . . . 'Who is dat? Aye, what do you?' No answer. By then the dog beside him began whining. When he got close enough, it was enough for a big man to mess himself. He said the man sat propped against the tree, back straight as if he was tied to it, the whole of his clothes covered in blood. The two eyeball almost out of the socket. The shout he started shouting, before he reach back out in the main road by under Kakaul, all Grand Roy and Mt. Plaisir people was running to meet him to find out what was wrong.

Aaye; one bacanal in the place. One caca cocoa. Police up

108

and down. Grenada police, Trinidad police. I don't know what they had to send for Trinidad police for. I'm sure our police just as good if not better. Anyway some people said the man killed himself, others said is people that killed him. One story that went round for a long time was that it was the man in Grenville who he fighting court house, although the man win the case. They said because he working with the devil police can't catch him. I don't understand all that; if the devil is so strong God must be stronger. So people who work with God must be stronger than those who work with the devil. That's what I think, anyway. They even say the lawyer had hand in the death.

The night of the wake Miss Endly bawled she bawled. She sat on the floor groaned, grunted, grunted and groaned. One minute she on the floor the next she jumped hoop hoop, boaw woye boaw. Jumped up a book, kook, took, took, boop, prancing about and bawling all kind of 'O Gawd papa bunjay'. She danced as if she had a whole army of African spirits in her. Poor Sheila. I felt so sorry for her. She did not know where she was. Her family came from Birchgrove and Grenville and all over the island, but her brothers and sister overseas did not come. Not for the funeral anyway. People always say when things happen it's hot news for only nine days, afterwards things cooled down.

But things were not the same with Sheila and her mother after that. They sort of given up. Sheila started missing school. Around the house was still tidy, but not the same. The flowers did not look pretty as before. Everything looked so sad. It was about a year later that that damn thief turned up saying he is preacher. Sheila left her good church and started following him quite down in Brizan, saying she see the light. Next thing she and Miss Endly left the village. Not a word to anybody, not even their neighbour. I always used to say Sheila was my best friend, but when she left she did not tell me self . . . not one word. I thought that she and her mother went overseas, perhaps to meet her sister or brother, but I heard the mother alone went to Trinidad and spend a little time, and Sheila ended up in Paradise with the preacher man.

Their house did not stay empty for long. One of her cousins moved in a little while after they left. Is a good thing too, because I wouldn't like to see the amount of bush that would of grown around the place. It don't take long for bush to make around the houses look like jungle at all. Look at the state of around Marcia and them house. They would be surprised when they come back. Only two months since they went to St. Vincent, only two months, and you would think is years. Not to say that they didn't used to clean the place. When they were home, bush didn't get the chance to say howdy. Marcia and her family lived in that house since before I born. It's a bit funny to see the house without light in the night. It's Marcia, her mother and brother that lived there now.

The older brother living in St. Vincent now. It's him they gone to spend time with. I don't really know him, because he never used to stay one place. A real sagaboy. Knocking about all over the place. Mammy say he was always like that since he was a teenager. Sometimes the poor mother don't know what corner of the globe he end up. The only thing she could do is pray for him. One time he found himself all the way up in Jamaica. Miss Verna must make the sign of the cross a hundred times when he decided to settle down, even if it was not in Grenada. Mammy said Calvin was a very nice young man, but a bit of a scamp as well as a drivey.

110

He almost send the mother in Richmond Hill once. Mammy was living on the other side at the time, but she remember when the bacanal broke out on Saturday morning. What happened was as usual Miss Verna got up, pack her things to go to the market to sell. She send Damon down the road ahead of her with a basket of things. He was supposed to wait until Marcia came and then go back for some more load. Two two as Damon reached down the road he was back, bawling all murder police. The boy was bawling for his mother and sister and running up the hill as if the devil was behind him. I was just born at the time, but I always hear Mammy talking about it. Apparently Tanty Clarice was by the road when it happened, so she told Mammy. The story was that in the dusky morning, while they were waiting for the bus, they noticed a car cruising down Cacoben Hill, then pull up outside Mr Errol shop. Nobody paid attention because they thought was somebody trying to make a few cents, you know trying to box brains to get one of them to hire to take their load to town. Anyway, as soon as Damon put down the basket, this girl rushed out of the car with a bundle in her hand which she tried to give the boy, just like that. Just tried to push this white bundle in the little boy hand. Before he could open his mouth she started cursing him and telling him to take it . . . take it. Everybody started gathering around the girl. Well; when Damon catch his breath he turned as if the wind was behind him. 'Mammy . . . Mammy . . . Marcia, O Gawd, Mammy, Mammy,' he called to his family.

He running up the hill, the girl running behind him. By this time the whole foreroad wake up. Was a good thing the bus was late because it would of left some people behind. Well talk about tabaye. Miss Verna that never in anything,

111

never tell anybody the eye black or white trouble come to meet her right in her house. She and her children was the best mannered people in the place. Mammy said from the time she know the lady, nobody could point a finger at she and her children. Even Calvin, no matter how he knockabout, he was one of the most respectable young man you ever met. No matter where he went whenever he came back he always do little jobs around the house for his mother before he take off again. His mother in the place as if she not there, but that Saturday morning things changed. When Marcia heard her little brother hollering she rushed down behind Miss Evelyn house. Her mother behind her. As Marcia turned below the lime tree she saw Damon running up and this person running behind him. Miss Elsie boy had followed Damon and the girl. When he saw Marcia he ran back down the road saying ruction was about to break out under the hill. He said he don't know what was going on but the sight of Marcia face in the early morning reminded him of guinea pepper.

Everybody started running mouth. Miss Elsie got worried because she and Miss Verna always travelled together on Saturday morning, and she don't know what's happening. The bus soon come and the other woman's load on the ground and nobody looking after it. She called to her friend and remind her the bus soon come. Miss Verna had no choice but to sent Marcia and Damon to town on their own. Was the first time she ever sent them by themselves, but she had no choice. That set more tongue on fire, especially when they noticed the girl ran back into the car without the bundle.

By nine o'clock the whole place was on fire. Mammy said she was real sorry for Miss Verna. Quite where the woman is minding her business, trouble come to meet her. She said

112

God work in a mysterious way for true, because the last person Miss Verna expected to see was her son, because he only left the Friday morning, and usually he don't turn up again for months. But as if God sent him, he was home before midday the Saturday morning. As if she smelled him below the lime tree, because before he put his foot in front the door she started quarrelling with him. Not only Miss Verna mouth you hearing, but a baby crying. Aye aye baby crying in the woman house. The bundle the girl tried to give Damon was a baby, and the bag she had on her shoulder was the baby things. I never hear anything like that in my life. Just imagine giving away your child like is a bundle of clothes. And the worse thing, Miss Verna didn't even know about any baby. The story was that Calvin had the child with a girl in Happy Hill. He didn't tell his mother, not even his sister about the child because the child mother told him she don't want his family to know about the baby. The time come now and she want to go to Trinidad, and her parents would not keep the child because they thought the child only have three months it's too young for the mother to leave it. She skin so hot, she wanted to go, that's when she decided to bring the child to Miss Verna.

Tanty Clarice said she don't know how Calvin managed to get the girl in the family way. These people and them so stuck up, they think because their skin look like mongoose, and their hair like coconut fibre that they better than other people. The thing is Calvin was a real sweet man, he knew how to sweet talk anybody. Anyway this girl must really be stupid to think she could keep a baby from the Mills family. These people can't loose. You only have to look at the eyes to know a person have the Mills blood in the body. Those eyes are like their trademark . . . very little eyelash or eye-

113

brow, but just eyeball . . . big and dark . . . and when they roll, they roll. Grace didn't want Calvin to tell his family about the baby, but she didn't think it wrong to dump her on Miss Verna that Saturday morning. the girl so stupid, she didn't have to do that, all she had to do was to bring the lady grandchild to her in the right way. The way she took her farseness and dump the child and then run, people would think that police was behind her. To tell you the truth I hear it's a good think she ran as well, because if Marcia did catch her she would of wished it was the police. Anyway Miss Verna got the story from Calvin. She gave him one dressing down. All he did was say how he sorry, very sorry. When she asked him why he didn't tell her about the child he said the mother told him not to say anything. He was just waiting, waiting for her to change her mind. He begged the mother to take the child. I don't know what he thought his mother would of done with the child. You only have to look at the little girl's eyes and then she had the birthmark like her father.

Strange how things could happen, one night Miss Verna had three in her family; by next morning she started buying baby milk, and not new new baby but three months old baby girl . . . everything settle down as normal. Hilary grew up with her grandmother in Grand Roy, but she also got to know her other grandparents in St. Davids. As for Grace, nobody heard anything from her for a long time. Once she sent Christmas card for Hilary, nothing else. Not even a birthday card until just before Hilary had 10. The child was growing with her grandmother nice nice. Who don't know the story would think she was Miss Verna youngest child, until Grace turn up saying she come to take her child to Trinidad with her. By that time her father was sort of living in St. Vincent. He still use to knockabout a bit, but he was more in St. Vincent than anywhere else. Anyway, Grace turned up saying she was married in Trinidad and she wants her child with her. She said her husband wants Hilary to live with them as a complete family. I never know anybody could be so brass. The woman brass than brasso. She turned up like hurricane Janet, saying she is the child mother and nobody can stop her from taking her child. She said she had all the papers ready for them to leave for Trinidad the next Wednesday. That only gave Miss Verna six days to do anything to stop her and it seemed hopeless. Mammy said everybody in the place was vex, real vex. Some remembered the day Grace dumped the baby on Miss Verna. Marcia was planning to give the woman a good beating when she came back in front their door, but her mother told her don't even think about. She said if the woman had the guts to come and put claim to the child, she is her mother and nobody could prevent her from taking her child.

Everybody was upset, especially Hilary, but there was nothing to do. All Miss Verna kept on saying was trust in God . . . He is a great Redeemer. Even the grandparents in Happy Hill could not do anything. Wednesday Grace came and took Hilary away with her grip and a few things. Miss Verna made sure Marcia and her brother was not home because she did not want any confusion. Tanty Clarice said all that morning they could hear Miss Verna singing hymn after hymn as if was only she and God in the world. Was about eleven o'clock Grace came with a car took the child and left. When Mammy repeated the story I was vex and sorry for the people as if it was Mammy it happened to. Imagine coming and taking the child just like that. The same way she dumped her like a parcel, the same way she come

115

and pick her up. Mammy said she remembered seeing them when they left. The child wasn't crying, but she was so sad she made you want to cry.

Well, Mammy usually say some strange things, but some things she says have meaning. A thing she always used to say is 'God works in a mysterious way his wonders to perform'. I don't know how to explain that, but what I know is that up to this day Miss Vera and her children, including Hilary her granddaughter, still live in the same house. I don't know all the story but apparently Hilary did not sleep out of her grandmother house for one night, not one single night. And her mother went back to Trinidad.

Coming back to the new people in Sheila's house, Mammy said the girl looked like Hilary. I don't find so at all. For one thing the girl look too stuck up for me. At a glance she reminded me of my sister Janice but close up it's different. The way she skinned up her face and look at me as if she smell mess or something, I don't even want to pass by her house. She skin like mongoose, she must be think she nice. I was glad that there were people living in the house, but that don't mean we must be friends. Mammy says it's good to have neighbours, but you don't have to be running inside their house all the time. The same way it's not good to let all kind of people in and out of your house. She says sometimes is pretending they pretending to be friends all the time is your business they peeping in to bring outside. When they sit down under the post office balcony, slapping sandflies plap plap and eating Mildred coconut tart, is people business they pounding. There is a set of people in the place everyday, day-in day-out they under the balcony. Morning noon and night they under the balcony. When they pound news all day, in the evening they get up, brush their hands across

116

their bam, go home and the next day they back again. When we lived by Miss Beverley it was like most houses, we run from one yard to the other. Little tracks all around the houses that people use for road. Some mornings as soon as we open our front door is Miss Beverley children we see going in the latrine to empty the tensil. They don't have no shame. Sometimes big bright day they have the tensil of pee sit down in front the door next to the basket of provision. That is one bad thing about having neighbours too near you.

But then again sometimes it's a good thing. Like the time that damn thief left all the way from Grand Mal and come to thief in Grand Roy. The man must of been drunk. He passed right in front of paren Joshua yard, say good morning to Miss Effie then went straight to Mr Man house to try and break it open. That's the brassiest thief I ever heard about in my life. When Miss Effie bawled out to him, asked him what the hell he think he doing, he had the nerve to turn round and say Mr Man was his uncle and he come to look after the house while his uncle gone oversea. He should of done his homework better.

When he said about Mr Man being his uncle was then Miss Effie really bawled. She let out one piece of 'Ah you oye look at my trouble, look at a damn thief breaking in my brother house'. She screamed out to paren Hacket. She just screamed and screamed how that damn thief come breaking in her brother house. Thief must make this man stupid or something, or perhaps lougarou suck the little blood he had in his head, because he would of known that Miss Effie is Mr Man sister. When paren Hacket heard the woman bawled out he grabbed the piece of bootoo he had behind the front door and ran outside. The same time Andrew was in his mother kitchen drinking his tea, he put the cup down, ran out shouting 'Whey is the thief, whey is him'. Everybody ran out of their house. Jacob didn't know where to run, he put foot up in Miss Agnes yard but the dogs were waiting for him. He cut across in Mr Cato yard, there he boot up on Mr Cato two boys. Well I tell you these boys held down the man, and with paren Hacket, Andrew and one or two others gave the man one beating. They almost half kill him. When they finished with him they dragged him to the police station.

He started making complain to the police, saying he only passing and those people started on him. The police did not even listen to him. Is a long time they were looking for him. Apparently he did the same thing down by Happy Hill, and way up in Concorde. The Concorde woman house he broke into reported it to the police, but they didn't catch him. So he thought he would try his luck nearer the police station. Old people have a saying: 'One day for thief, one day for watchman.' Was a good thing is Miss Effie who saw him. Imagine trying to tell the woman he is her own brother nephew when she know was only two children her parents had.

Was a good thing the houses were near by each other. But it's not always good to be so close. Like when we were in the other place, the people below us was so nasty, sometimes when we were sitting in front the door is the time they going in the latrine with tensil. That's not all; people used to take our front yard for main road. If they wanted to go up by Miss Vero instead of making the round by the Pentecostal church, they make track under the lime tree behind our kitchen. The way everybody passing there as if they change the main road. It's different down by Miss Evelyn, although the road – a little track really – although it pass between her

118

house and her kitchen, there's nothing she can do about it because it is the allow road; that's how the plan worked out. Mammy says is damn stupid people that sell out land and work out main road in front other people door.

Sometimes Miss Evelyn making coconut oil or bully bakes, big big blaze of fire from the fireside, smoke thick as when people burning corn land, yet people passing there shaking their skin over the woman things. One day one bacanal broke out. One thing in the place. It was the time Miss Madonna was sick in bed. Sick – that was another thing. They said the woman sick bad, all doctor her family called they couldn't find anything wrong with her. No change. They called the Catholic priest to pray for her. They called the Seventh Day Adventist priest to pray for her . . . no change. They even called Pastor Myer from the Church of God in Two Rock . . . still no change . . . All priest, all doctor, no change in the woman's condition. The day the bacanal with Miss Evelyn and Miss Saydo broke out was the day the Catholic priest went to prayer for the sick woman. I hear the man looked at the woman shaking on the bed and he almost ran out of the room.

George, that my godmother little boy, was there. He said just before the priest came Miss Madonna was very quiet. They thought she was sleeping. The daughter even told the priest that her mother was catching a rest. She said she was glad because the old woman hardly close her eyes. The priest said that was alright. He said he would sit by her bed quietly and prayer. Aye aye as soon as the man pushed his head behind the blind he noticed something twisting twisting on the bed under the sheet like a big snake. Not just the twisting but a kind of blabbering noise was coming from underneath the sheet as well. God-fearing man or not he was frightened.

119

At first he could not see any head, then a little dry head poked out, just the top. Then the hands came out moving like when the headmaster conducting his choir. The priest didn't know what to do. George said he was on the big stone by the side of the house watching at what was going on inside. He said he supposed the priest usually prayer with people who had the devil in them, but he never met up that kind of devil before. Perhaps he was praying for Miss Saydo to join him.

While he was at Miss Madonna, Miss Saydo was on her way to meet him in truth. She left her house well dressed with her bible under her arm, you would think she was going to church. She could of passed on the other side by the church but instead she passed in front Miss Evelyn door. As she reached under the window, splish splash Miss Evelyn threw out a bowl of fresh jacks water. Woy o yoye, things start. Miss Saydo bawled out how Miss Evelyn spiteful. She saw her under the window and because she don't have God in her she wet her with the jacks water. She called Miss Evelyn an old jezeebel. Told her she is the devil incarnate. All kinds of things. All how Miss Evelyn saying sorry, it's an accident, Miss Saydo didn't believe her. She called the woman an old liar. Well they shouted at each other, called each other all kind of names. One ruction in the place. Then Miss Evelyn came outside ready to fight. She picked up a piece of burn wood from the fireside and raised her hand to hit Miss Saydo. Miss Saydo held up the bible to hit the other woman. Before they actually hit each other, George called Miss Saydo and told her that the priest waiting for her up by Miss Madonna. When he heard the noise he left where he was to see what was happening. Then something run in his mind to tell Miss Saydo about the priest being in the sick

120

woman house. That was how she stopped quarrelling and went to meet the priest. But people don't forget easily, you know; up to now they still call Miss Saydo fishwater.

One day she went and dip her mouth in Estelle business. The thing was, everybody knew about Estelle and the new policeman. They were saying things like how Estelle in the police station late late in the night with the police. Some even say they see her leaving the station early in the morning. Perhaps was not even true, but you know how people farse. They only have to see two people talking to start running their mouth.

Like the time Miss Freeman saw me and teacher Stanley, the Catholic teacher, walking on Douglastone Bridge. I had about 15. Me and teacher Stanley was actually waiting for his sister Myrna who was at her friend's house by the river. I was waiting for her because she had my homework exercise. Her brother was in the park watching a football match. When I told him where she was he said he would wait for her. We were walking, talking and laughing. I can't even remember what we were talking about. Miss Freeman came from Gouyave going to La Poutree. As she reached us she said, 'Evening Flora. You doh go down yet! Come on we go make good company.' She said all that before I opened my mouth. All the while she talking she looking at teacher Stanley.

'I waiting for a friend, Miss Freeman. I catch up with you just now.'

'Awright saye saye,' she said. 'You young people eh, you young people.' She looked in my eyes as if she putting jumbie on me. Then she turned to teacher Stanley, the bad eye she gave him. Well if looks could of killed he was as dead as a dead herring. Two days later Mammy asked me why I was late the other evening. I told her again. I was waiting for

121

Myrna. She had my homework exercise. She asked if Myrna started wearing trousers and tie. Then she began preaching again. How those force ripe boys only after one thing. She said how Miss Freeman saw me and that Stanley man hug up on Douglastone Bridge. I couldn't even open my mouth to say it was not true. I couldn't turn and call Miss Freeman a liar, because I know is a beating I would get. Believe me, I was so vex I felt the birthmark on my shoulder scratching me. Mammy went on about how those damn little boys think them is man. They look down, see two little hair roots peeping out between their leg they think that make them man. They only after people daughters to spoil them. When she start to quarrel like that, I just keep my mouth close because I know what I will get. From then I know I had to watch myself. Miss Freeman lie so much fancy saying she see me and teacher Stanley hug up.

I didn't even like the man. He was nothing like Alvin. Alvin was . . . well he was nice. He was an acolyte in our church. When he have on his nice bright white surplice on the altar on Sundays he look handsome. Teacher Stanley was nothing like him. That's just to show how people could make up things. They saying all kind of things about Estelle and the policeman. The man only used to be in the station sometimes two days a week. Perhaps the times they saying he and Estelle in the station he not even in the village. I remember he was a very friendly person. I was very small but he used to make little joke with all the children. Once people see two persons talking and they can't find out what they talking about they making mischief. The same way they almost break up teacher Marion and teacher Bennett with their bad mouth. Was a good thing he was not as stupid as they think. He knew who started to spread the stories. He knew was jealous the girl who started spreading news about teacher Marion was jealous. The girl mother tried for a long time to get him interested in her daughter. He used to talk to the girl but he said was nothing in it. He was only being friendly, but the girl and her mother took it more serious. When he and teacher Marion got engaged and thing, the girl started saying things about teacher Marion. Was a good thing the teachers had more sense than to bother with what people say.

Anyway, the day Miss Saydo and Estelle catch up in the foreroad, I don't know what the woman was thinking about. Everybody 'fraid Estelle mouth. Miss Saydo went to full her bucket of water. She saw the policeman leaning over the balcony talking to Estelle. I don't know how it really happened, but Miss Saydo mentioned how all man that come in the place Estelle shaking she frock tail for them. Estelle turned and called her 'fish water'. Was then real tabaye started. If the policeman hadn't left the balcony and come in the road to stop them was fight that was about to break out. Next morning early early Miss Saydo got up saying she going to Gouyave to take out summons against Estelle and the policeman for assault. When she reached Boawden gap she started counting to Papa JoeJoe, about how the two people assaulted her, and she going take them to court. Papa JoeJoe told her she wasting her time and money, she could never win policeman in front magistrate. The next thing we heard was the woman started going up in Grenville to the man in the pease. The woman saying she is a good Christian woman. Everyway the priest went she behind him holding up his surplice, with heavy heavy bible under her arm. Yet as soon as night come or before day break she taking her money to people to work nastiness.

Mammy says when you see these don't wash their hand, in the end they always suffer. Is true true. One minute Miss Saydo strong and healthy doing her work and thing next minute she gone blind in one eye. Not only that, she had a little scratch on her foot around her ankle; she said was a piece of rope that bruised her. Little by little the bruise grew into a sore. Now she have a big sore foot, nothing in the doctor shop could dry it up. My grandmother is another one for her old fashion sayings. She used to say when these people worked with the devil after a while he wants his pay; nothing in this life is for nothing.

Anyway going back to what I was saying about the woman and little girl that moved into Sheila house. It's nice to have neighbour, especially when they are not too close to each other, but somehow that girl looked too stuck up for me. When I went home I told Mammy about how friendly the woman was, but the girl looked at me as if she smelled something. Mammy laughed. She said I'm always finding fault with people, but she would be surprised if we don't become friends soon. Friends; I don't know about that. For one thing she looks a bit younger than me and the other I just don't like stuck up people. They go on as if they don't breathe the same air as everybody else. I remember once Mammy and Miss Chrissie was talking about the woman who played the organ in the church. I wasn't listening to their talk, but I heard when Miss Chrissie let out one long 'Chupes'. Then she said 'The woman go on like she mess don't stink'. I burst out one laugh. I wasn't supposed to be listening but sometimes you can't help hearing when big people talking. 'As if she mess don't stink!' – that's the funniest thing I heard for a long time. Well, this stuck up girl reminded me of that; perhaps she thinks she mess don't stink.

Mammy seemed to know things before they happened. I don't know how she knew me and the girl would be friend, but is true. About three months after they moved in, Gloria invited me to her birthday party and I really enjoyed myself. Although she looked a lot younger than me I only had one year more than her. Since after the party we became good friends. Since Sheila left I did not have a best friend, so it was nice to have to talk little secrets with. Not everything but some secrets. In some ways me and Gloria was very alike, we always found things to laugh about, but sometimes she take things too serious. She was funny like that. Not funny to laugh at but strange funny. Some times I don't know how to make a joke with her, because she go on like an old woman. Once I made a joke and call her grandma, the girl vex vex you would think is curse I cursed her. Because we go to the new school in Florida sometimes on Saturdays, we have to go to the school or even the church to practise for something or the other, like practising in the choir for the wedding, although she was not in the wedding choir. One Saturday morning we were going to choir practice in the church in Gouyave. It was practice for the procession for All Saints' Night. Anyway it was getting late. We always left home about eight o'clock to walk up; sometimes we get a lift but most times is walk we walk. I always like to leave home early so we don't have to rush rush because I know what the headmaster is like; when he says eight he means eight, not one minute past. That morning Gloria turned so much it was getting later and later. I was praying that we would get a lift by the post office van but was a new driver that morning; he past us like exam. When we reached by the park, we already late, but instead of hurrying Gloria

125

started quarrelling to herself and dragging her foot. I heard her say 'Chupes' so I asked what was wrong.

'She must be playing bright!' Gloria answered, cutting eyes at a girl who passed us.

'Bunjay what you talking about? Who playing bright?!' I asked.

'Dat old ugly girl nuh. She pass; looked at me in the poke of my eyes and don't even say howdy, as if she don't know me.'

'Gloria what you talking about? Perhaps the girl don't know you! Maybe she just look like somebody you know. People could look like each other, you know. One day I went and pull this man shirt sleeve because I thought was my uncle.'

'Chupes. You think I stupid or something? I know her. I know her good. Is she.'

'Well perhaps she didn't make you out.' I tried to calm her down, because by that time she was well vex.

'What you mean she don't make me out? How come I know she, eh? How come I make she out? Bright she playing bright.'

'Aye aye girl you could vex easy oui! The girl pass, she don't call you, you have to get vex for that! Come let's walk fast, it's getting late.'

Sometimes I don't understand Gloria at all. One minute she vex, the next she start laughing. Laughing in the road like she funny in her head. I couldn't see what she was laughing at. I turned my eyes cross way to look at her. When she was vex a few minutes before her nose was perspiring. When she started laughing there were creases of sweat underneath her eyes. I didn't have time to argue with her; we only had a few minutes to get to the church and before that I had

126

to go up on the Lance to see if I get some candles for Mammy to put on our dead people graves. The year before I had to go quite in town to search for candles on the last minute. We thought that we were going to get two packets from Miss Molly, but she sold out. When I said to Mammy that we could borrow one or two she was very upset, not vex – kind of sad. She said since she know herself, two things her mother never borrowed, candle to put on our people graves and salt. She said her mother never done it and she Mammy have no intention to do it in her life, especially now she getting old. She had something about getting old. The way she speak you would think she already reached her three scores and ten. She said if once a year we can't put ourselves out to clean up our family graves and burn a few candles, that shows how much we loved them when they were alive. She says if you have to borrow, that shows you have no respect for the dead.

The salt story is different. Apparently a woman shows her true value by always having salt in the home. I don't really understand these customs. I believe some of them came from Africa when our great great great great grandparents were brought to the Caribbean. Things like the shango dances and making salacca. When I had 13 Miss Mildred over the river made a big shango dance. It was bigger than the one cousin Melda made for Boca. This time was about three bus load that came down from Grenville. They came with their drums, flutes, shak shaks and things. Their clothes were the big wide floral African gowns. They spent three nights and days, singing, dancing, chanting and playing their music. The women looked so nice in their clothes. For each gown they had a head tie to match. I was only able to watch them in the daytime. I would of liked to go to the meetings in the night because that was when the real dance and music take place, but Mammy said she don't believe in all that African stupidness so she won't let me go. In the daytime when I pass by the house and see them, I feel sort of nice . . . sort of drawn to them. I could feel as if the spirit was talking to me. I didn't tell anybody how I felt, especially Mammy because I know she would tell me to go to confession. I am sure this thing about always having salt in the house was passed down from slavery times. People still believe in it, although the true meaning might be a bit corrupted.

Once there was a shortage of salt in the island. There was some kind of trouble in the salt mines somewhere in Bequia, I believe, so the workers went on strike. While everybody was running about begging for a grain of salt, Mammy had how much packets in a box under the dresser in the kitchen. She gave some to our close friends like Miss Chrissie and my grandmother and aunts. One day I asked her what would happen if the strike not over and our salt run out.

'Lawd,' I said. 'Mammy, imagine people eating food without salt everyday. Boy o boy lougarou would really have a good time.' She laughed. Screwed up her face and pammed her lips, like she keeping a secret. Her high cheek bone shining fat and brown like a new two cents piece. She squinted her eyes. The thick eyelids sort of closed over the eyelash, making you think her eyes are closed. Sort of trying to make them smaller. She always make me laugh when she does that.

'What you doing, Mammy?' I teased. 'Making up your face as if you hiding a secret or something.'

She spread her lips in a broad smile. Turned her head towards town and shook it as if telling me something. I didn't understand what she was on about and knew better

128

than asking any questions at that time. After the strike over about a week later she gave me the story. She said Tanty Floris does send little salt and saltfish for us from Trinidad by the trafficking boat. The man on the boat was some family to us, so he used to bring the things over. He had to be careful though, because if they caught him is big big trouble for him.

Coming back to the Saturday morning when Gloria got vex because some girl or the other didn't call her. Well I didn't have time to play in any stupidness with her, so I decided to hurry leaving her behind if she don't hurry. It was getting late and I wanted to get the candles. Mammy used to make sure and buy the candles week before All Saints' Day, but last year and this year she told me to buy them. Last year I left it for the last minute, thinking I was going to get some by Miss Molly. Because was All Saints' all people who don't usually buy candles buy them up, so when went for some Miss Molly sold out. That's the only time of the years some people bother to go in a cemetery unless they going to funeral. But it's nice to see how the churchyard and cemetery clean up nice nice. I wish people won't leave the place a whole year to clean. Some don't even bother. They forget they have family buried in the cemetery or churchyard. Big All Saints' Night not even a candle they would burn to shine a light for the dead. Mammy says some people is the devil walking on earth. They don't have respect for God, they don't have respect for the dead. She says remembering the dead on All Saints' and All Souls' Nights is a tradition, and if people not careful that will be forgotten.

When she says things like that I think more about the Grenville people making the shango dances. These people don't forget about Africa, I used to say to myself. Mammy would say things like people would forget their own souls. Some of them go to church once a year, at Christmas and that's only to show off their new clothes. On Christmas Eve night and Christmas morning, the church pack. Everybody dress up in their new, white clothes looking like angels, but look in some of their faces is pure Satan you seeing. All how they try to cover up, they can't cover up their wickedness. Still they bowing their heads low low, playing innocent. Cocking up their bottoms high high in the air, walking as if they can't marsh ants, say they going to the altar for communion. Sometimes I wish the Host would choke them or the wine go down their wrong throat. When I look at some of them on the altar, I feel sorry for the priest. It must be hard for him after listening to their confessions, knowing how wicked some of them are and still have to give them communion. The penance they do after confession could never be enough to wash away their sins. After that one confession, their feet don't see the church door again until the next December, not even on Good Friday. Not even on All Saints' Night to burn a candle. Some of the graves is nothing but bush; not even a wood cross to mark the spot. I don't know what happen to people in their head. No wonder Mammy says them is nothing but Satan, Satan walking God earth like man.

Talking about the cemetery and the graves, I hope that this year is better than last year. As this year All Saints' fall on a Saturday, anything could happen when those drunkard leave the rum shop, saying they have the spirit in them. The only spirit they have in them is white rum, then they don't have respect for the living or the dead. I remember when Mr Magnus died. Funeral service going on in the church.

130

Everybody sad. Some, especially the family, crying. People had to hold up Miss Magnus and her daughter.

The priest was reading the lesson, then all of a sudden one noise broke out in front the church door. The voice like some old cow bawling in the slaughter house. The next thing we heard was people singing inside the church, but towards the back. One man singing 'Woy a yoye me donkey want water . . . hold him Joe', and another shouting, 'Show me de way to go home . . . I'm tired and want to go to bed.' When I heard the first 'Woy o yoye', I thought was somebody bawling for the dead, but when the rest came out, well I don't know, really don't know. They right inside the church under the bell. I suppose priest not supposed to be vexed or at least show when they vex, but Father Ryan was vex. With these people, even though they don't say anything you know when they are angry. Father Ryan whole face became red like the flambouyant tree. He stopped the service and went to talk to Jacob and his partner. They said they were celebrating. Up to now no body knows what they were celebrating. I don't know what Father Ryan said to them, but the next Sunday Jacob was in church. Was the first time I see Jacob in collar and tie, let alone inside a church. Not only that; soon afterwards he started taking lessons for confirmation. The children used to tease him – a big old man like that was not confirmed. I don't know if he ever went through with it but Father Ryan did a good job on Jacob.

I wish he was in Coastguard cemetery last year All Saints' Night when we went to put candles on cousin Lisa and the others' graves. As I'm always saying, some people don't have respect, not even for the dead. I know people forget their dead and things like that, but last year I think even the dead people in their graves must have cried because of loneliness.

131

The cemetery is on a large, square slope overlooking the sea. Before time, when people really cared about their dead on All Saints' Night, when you stay in the main road and look up at the cemetery, when the graves are covered in lighted candles, it looked like a square Christmas tree, especially on a dark night. Anyway last year was the worse, only four families went to the graves, we and three others. A stranger looking at the cemetery would think it was planned the way it was only the four corners of the cemetery that was lighted. All our dead families were in one corner of the cemetery, the far corner at the top. We could look down the slope at the other graves. Cousin Ann, me, Cynthia and Devon were at cousin Lisa's grave. While we lighted the candles, cousin Ann was praying and we answering as we went on.

After a while we heard a sort of scarey noise, like whiish, shuishy, ghosty coming from the middle of the cemetery. There were stories about certain people buried there. They say some of them worked with the devil when they were alive, so their souls cannot rest in peace. They talked about a woman and her son. Apparently he killed her and then killed himself, or could be the other way around. Whatever way it was, it was not natural deaths. People said the family was the devil disciples. They said these people had big business. They were rich rich, but it was funny how they got their riches. They were ordinary poor people. Working hard to send their children to school, then all of a sudden they became big shot. People noticed they had even stopped going to church. Whatever; way they got their riches, people reckoned it was evil, especially when most of the family ended up bad. They say long after the mother and son dead and buried, you could hear them crying in the cemetery. That happened a long time ago, but people still talk.

We used to think was old time story, but when we heard that ghosty ghosty noise, I started thinking about these things. To make matters worse, while we doing our business all of a sudden Cynthia bawled out 'Ah you oye look, look down dey. Look look.' I thought the first noise frightened me; well I tell you I didn't know what 'fraid was. Cousin Ann sort of stopped and start and stop and start her praying. I was trying to listen to her, but my eyes were on what was happening in the middle of the cemetery. Cousin Ann said she not afraid of dead people because she is protected. I'm not sure about that. Instead of saying three 'Hail Mary', she said two. Stopped, started 'Our Father', and mixed it up with another 'Hail Mary'. Me and Cynthia trying to follow the prayers, but it was difficult. Our eyes were glued to this thing in the middle of the cemetery. This big ball of fire was hopping from grave to grave and dancing. One minute it was on one grave, the next it sort of rolled in the air on to another. All the while making that strange, ghosty noise as if calling and not calling. Cousin Ann was pretending she brave, but after a few minutes she was really mixing up the 'Our Father' and 'The Lord is my Shepherd'. Me, I was peeing myself. True. I squeezed my legs tight but I could still feel the hot pee running down my legs. My panty was wet. Cynthia was holding my hand as if it was part of her body. After a few minutes somebody from the other side shouted out: 'Lougarou; ah you doh see lougarou in the burial ground.' Cynthia grabbed me around my waist; Devon hugged on to my other side. My free hand fly around cousin Ann neck. I tell you if that lougarou passed by us it couldn't find a breeze between us. I could feel cousin Ann and Cynthia clothes wetty wetty with sweat. I was wondering if they peed themselves as well. With all that cousin Ann still pre-

133

tending she not frightened, even though she mixing up all the prayers.

One of the families who was lighting candles in one corner of the burial ground started shouting out: 'Lougarou, lougarou!' Another one bawled out 'Ah you oye look at me trouble nuh. People doh sleeping, yet lougarou come out.' Believe me, by this time my head was like a dry boli full of seeds. A real boli, shak shak, only difference was that the seeds were big stones knocking my temples boaw, boaw, boaw. Was a good thing it was night and nobody could see my face. The way my eyes were popping out of my head was sure to make them 'fraid.

'Cousin Ann let's go.' Cynthia said. 'Come on.'

'Yeh; let's go, Cousin Ann. I 'fraid,' Devon added.

'Come on,' I joined in.

Cousin Ann carried on with her half prayers and trying to light the candles that blow out. By that time the lougarou had company. Instead of one ball of fire there were about four, and they had changed tactics. Instead of rolling about or hopping on the graves, they were opening and closing yap yap yippy yip yap as if they had wings. Opening and closing. Hopping and rolling about. They did a little dance on one grave, rolled over, then did something else on another.

'Cousin Ann, come on. Let's go,' Cynthia repeated.

'Cousin Ann let's go home. The candles awright. They could burn by themself. Let's go.' I urged. We forget the real reason we were there. We just wanted to get out of the place and go home. The other people lighted whatever candles they managed and left the place. Yak a tak tak, yak a tak, we heard their voices as they ran from the burial ground. Everybody seemed to have gone, leaving us with these things.

Then, just as cousin Ann started another round of 'Hail Mary', she broke out with one piece of 'You all damn thief . . . look those damn thief.'

I almost jumped on Cynthia back. The lighted candle in my hand went out phewep. It was a good thing those on the graves stayed lighting. When cousin Ann shouted, we freeze. The little group of us mus have looked like one black rock.

'Aaye lougarou! What lougarou?!' Cousin Ann kept on shouting 'Damn thief. All you leave the people candles alone. All you think all you could make me 'fraid, eh, that's what all you think. This early time, it don't even make dark good yet, all you come with damn stupidness making people believe you is lougarou. You ever see lougarou flying before people go to bed eh? Whey you ever see that? All you too damn thief. Leave the people candle alone.'

When we looked where the other people had left their candle burning yip yip yip, the candles were going out . . . quick quick one by one. While cousin Ann quarrelling, somebody in the middle of the burial ground shouted out: 'You people too stupid. You have money to burn.'

'What you mean? Eh, what you mean?' cousin Ann challenged the person. 'You too damn thief. What you don't go and look for work. All you so thief, you thiefing the dead.'

'Chupes. You people too stupid. You have money to burn,' the other person repeated, then added: 'What's the use burning light for dead people? They should burn their own light when they were alive. Burning candles for them now won't make them go in Heaven. Some so wicked God don't want them and the devil have sulphur put aside to send them to make their own hell, because he don't want them in his hell ah fus they bad. Give living people the money to buy bread.'

135

'Why you don't go and find work, eh find work to do? All you too thief and lazy.' Cousin Ann was making sure she had the last word. Those thieves let go some dirty words and ran out of the cemetery. After that we couldn't prayer properly. The candles were burning down, so cousin Ann agreed to go home and burn the rest of the candles in front the door. While we going home, cousin Ann was really quarrelling. Quarrelling as if she and somebody in confusion. She said those boys in the cemetery is nothing but the devil incarnate. How their mother should teach them manners. Teach them to have respect for people, especially the dead. She was vex boy. I mean vex. To me and Cynthia and the others, it was the best joke we had in a long time, especially the part where cousin Ann shouted out 'Damn thief' in the middle of the 'Hail Mary'. When we dropped off Devon, me and Cynthia started singing. When I say 'Hail Mary', Cynthia came in with 'You damn thief!' then we changed around. Cousin Ann stopped us. She said we blaspheming. That was the biggest joke of the year, although I believe people should respect the dead or leave others to get on with their thing.

I was thinking about these things as me and Gloria rushed to rehearsal. I didn't hear she was talking to me, until I felt she poked me on me shoulder.

'Flora, Flora.'

'What?'

'Aye, aye. I talking to you, you playing deaf. You face like you dreaming or something. What you thinking about?'

'Nothing. I was studying what happened in the cemetery last year. Remember I did tell you how those boys came playing lougarou just to thief the candles!'

'Aaye. You still studying that stupidness? Don't let those

136

vagabone and them bother you. I was thinking about the exams.'

'I don't bother about them exams. Is only geometry I don't like, but the other subjects should be easy.' Gloria fixed her eyes in my face as if she seeing somebody else.

'What you talking about Flora? What geometry you on about? You forget what teacher Anna said to us last week. I not talking about any geometry exam.' I had no idea what she was talking about.

Gloria was that sort of person. She start talking about one thing then go into something completely different in one breath. Even something that you never hear about in the first place, and then she call you stupid. Sometimes she reminds me of my grandmother. When the old lady was sick, sick in bed she was strange. Once she was real bad, everybody saying Ma Tan going to meet her Maker at last. People used to pass by the house, saying they coming to see Ma Tan for the last. One evening Miss Peters came to pray by the sick bed. That time Ma sick, flat down in bed. Mammy and Uncle Kenneth talking about what kind of coffin they would get for her. Anyway, Miss Peters said prayers from the prayer book, then asked Ma to repeat the Lord's Prayer after her. One minute she following Miss Peters good good, the next she go into her own conversation. When Miss Peters said 'Give us this day our daily bread', instead of repeating it, Ma started arguing with somebody called Tan Terese for a piece of land in Birchgrove.

Mammy said that Tan Terese was Ma Tan father sister. When the old man died he left a piece of nutmeg land for his daughter, but his sister did not give it up. All the time my grandmother strong on her two foot, I never hear her talk about land in Birchgrove. I know we had family up

137

there, but nothing about land. Not until she had 92 and on her death bed that these things come out. Not only about the land, but a whole load of things. One time Mammy made me and my cousins leave the room because she did not want us to hear what Ma was saying, especially when she started on about a boy she went to school with and what happened under a mango behind the school latrine. When she started talking about that person she started laughing. Laughing loud loud to herself. Quick quick Mammy pushed us outside. All how they tried to make the old woman hush she mouth, they couldn't. I don't know what was worse, the night she was running her mouth or what she used to do before she took to her bed . . .

Mammy say when people get old they go back into being children. She said their minds go back in time. I believe that to be true because of some of the things my grandmother did and said. One day me and her alone was in the house. I had about 11 that time. Mammy left me to look after her. To make sure she had something to eat and to see that she don't leave the house. That was another thing; we had to watch her. Watch her every minute of the day, otherwise she go walking. She used to go astray. The thing was she knew how to box brains. She would sit inside the room quiet quiet as if she resting, and when we not paying her mind she would creep out of the house by the back door and go. Just walk away in any direction her mind tell her, but usually up in the bush. Once we found her on the piece of land where she used to work in Mileqeize. She was moving about under the campeche tree, busy busy. When they found her she said she gathering wood to put a pit of coal on the fire. She on about how the people selling a tin of coal so dear, and Christmas coming it will be worse. They had one amount of

138

trouble to get her to come home. Uncle Kenneth and Mammy had to pretend they were people she used to work the land with. Talk in funny voices. They told her they put the coal on fire and it will burn alright. I cried. Although it was funny to hear my mother and uncle pretending they were other people, still it was not funny at all. It was sad to see how other people was shaking their heads, being sorry not only for my grandmother but for the whole family.

My grandmother had some funny ways, she did strange things before she died, but I really loved her. She made the sweetest coconut cakes and fudge in the village. All school children around the place grew up on Ma Tan fudge and coconut turnover. She used to sit under the red plum tree in the gap by the government school. She had a glass case with fudge and coconut cakes on the stone and a tray with coconut tart and turnover on her lap. Even when she about 80 she still used to sell her things. She only stopped when she had a bad sore foot after she bounced her foot on a stone in front the door . . . The sore foot did not stop her from wandering. Once when she walked away we searched everywhere for her. The whole village turned out looking for her. Fishermen blew shells all over the place. No Ma Tan. Police came and joined the search. Me and Mammy bawling. My uncles and aunts bawling. Women in the village bawling. No Ma Tan. Dark night falling, still no sight of the old lady. That night it was like a wake in the house. No body closed their eyes. Next morning I don't know how Francis managed to see her down in the stone hole by the bay going towards Black Bay. No body understand how she got down in this bad place with all these big rocks. Francis was going to his piece of corn land by the bay when he noticed the person under the sea side grapes trees. She was soaking wet. He called, but she did not answer. He ran back and raised the alarm.

I don't want to go on about my grandmother, but as I said Gloria reminded me so much of her. People say when you die you come back in another form, even as another person. Sometimes I think Gloria is really Ma Tan, but I know that can't be true because when Gloria was born Ma Tan was still alive. I don't know; I suppose that somehow some young people have some kind of old brain inside their head, and on the other hand when people get old their brain sort of mix up. Look how teacher Marion grandmother bawled out at the wedding. I know the old lady since I small. All of us used to do little things for her. If shell blowing in the foreroad she would send us to buy fish and sometimes wait for the bread van to buy bread for her. Sometimes if she not well a child would sleep with her, just to keep her company in the night.

She had a piece of land over the river; when planting season and everybody making maroon she used to make maroon too, to cut her corn land. Mammy used to send me to help her carry water and things. Miss Gracelyn used to make some stiff dumpling, Lawd. The dumpling as big as the ones Uncle Andrew and his mates used to cook carnival time. When she start sharing food, little or big, she give you a big bowl of food. I liked that. You eat until you feel you belly ready to bust.

One year me, Everest and his sister Veda went to help Miss Gracelyn with her maroon. She sent us back to the house for something. We crossed the river by under the big hog plum tree. The plums were riping. Big, yellow plums covered the ground like lino. Because was dry season we knew it would be alright to pass there, but if it was raining

140

it would be bad. When the rain fall and soak up the plums the place get swampy like in mango season, and there is that sort of sicky sweet smell. Although it's a plum and it look like the big St. Vincents plums, only difference is its inside is hairy and it's not goot to eat. Anytime those greedy children eat them; the next thing you hear them crying with belly pain, especially if the sun hot. That day when Miss Gracelyn sent us back to the house, sun was splitting earth. Veda so greedy. Before we left the garden Miss Gracelyn made sure we had our food. She gave us a big bowl of pigeon pease soup with dumpling, salt beef and things with a cup of juice to wash it down. We going good good, but Veda so greedy she said she want to taste the plum. All how me and Everest tell her not to put the thing in her mouth she don't hear. She had the first one, then she ate about three more, saying they taste nice. Not one but four, next thing she started holding her belly. Before we reached the bridge behind Mr Eli house she said she want to mess. Me and Everest started to laugh. Quick, quick she had to run in Mr Eli latrine. When she catch up with us she was really crying with her belly. She said it sort of cutting up inside and her face was sort of twisting. Everest did not say anything, but I knew he was worried, especially when Veda started saying how her eyes getting dark and she seeing things dancing in front her.

'We tell you not to eat the plum. You doh hear,' Everest said. 'We tell you, you know. Me and Flora cautioned you. You so greedy, you stuff yourself.' While he talking, I looking at Veda face. Even in the hot sun with perspiration running down her face, it looked as if she rubbed with ashes.

'Whey hurting you?' I asked. 'Only you belly?'

141

She nodded. 'And me head,' she whispered that I hardly hear her.

'Whey? You whole belly?' I was beginning to be frightened. Veda had a big mouth and now she can hardly open it. I was thinking because of her greediness she would get me and Everest in trouble. Anyway it was not too bad in the end; she only suffered a little bit. Because as soon as she reached her house and we told her mother, she got a dose of castor oil with vermafuse. Served her right. That would teach her not to be so greedy next time. When we went back and told Miss Gracelyn, she really laughed. She is alright. We didn't mind going to her house. Nobody expected her to bawl out in church, though. Could she be getting like my grandmother.

7

That old lady was something. True. The day the two of us was alone in the house, I was in the kitchen making something for us to eat. She was inside very quiet. The next thing I heard was her talking to somebody, telling the person to 'Put it on. Put it on so.' I went round by the front to have a look. Well I tell you I didn't know what to do. I was so frightened. Frightened and afraid. I was also ashamed because I wasn't supposed to see a big person in that way. I didn't know a lot about these things, although I started about three months before. Big people don't tell you things clearly. When it started, I thought I was the worse little girl in the world. Mammy explained things to me. I said I understand, but to tell you the truth I didn't understand at all – but I did not want to ask any questions because I still thought something was wrong with me and any minute she would give me a beating. I kept thinking and thinking of all the things I did that cause me to be passing blood. One day I heard my cousin Iris talking to her friend about 'the ting'. I pretended I wasn't listening because I thought because they bigger than me they would shout at me. When the friend left I asked Iris about and she told me things that made me feel better. From then I know it's women secret, but not women as old as my grandmother.

When I went to see what she was doing I was shocked. Ma was kind of cocked up on the floor; her frock tail tucked up in her waist and she had a piece of cloth in her hand. She was telling the person called Jessie to 'fold it so. Not so. Just so.' While she saying that she was folding the piece of cloth like a diaper. 'Put it on so,' she was saying. 'So. Don't be stupid. Look what I doing. Jessie, look at me. And don't let Caryle juke you.'

By this time she had lifted her petticoat and putting the diaper between her legs. I didn't know what to do. I just stand there with my mouth opened. I was shocked because Ma didn't even have on her drawers. I never seen my grandmother bottom, let alone her front. All the time she doing what she was doing she talking to that Jessie. I ran behind the house and peeped in a hole under the back room window. When she finished what she was doing she put on her drawers and pulled down her clothes. Sat on the chair with her pipe as if nothing happened. I said to myself I wouldn't tell anybody what I saw, but I wasn't staying in the house with her again on my own. When Mammy came home I told her Ma too miserable I can't look after her. She makes me too tired. Mammy looked at me as if she knew something had happened that I didn't want to talk about. I think was because she found the piece of cloth folded like a diaper in the corner. Mammy said she know the old lady miserable. Was not as she get old she like that, though she getting worse. She said when she and the others were little and Ma teaching them prayers, she would be telling them what to do the next day the same time as teaching them to pray.

Gloria was like that. Start telling me something and when

144

I answer or say something, she would be on something completely different in the same breath. One day I told her how she just like my dead grandmother. The way she looked me I thought she was vex, but she smiled her funny little smile. Sort of twist one corner of her bottom lip. Then she said perhaps she is my grandmother. Or a family. I know that was a joke because anybody who knows my family, especially on my mother side, would make us out easily. The velvet black skin. Those broad nose and big, bold bright eyes only belong to our family, no matter how far back. I said that to Gloria, even telling her the difference in our hair. She said I too stupid. Because she had straight hair don't mean anything, she got her from her father. She always calling people stupid. When you test her out she was more stupid than anything, although I know sometimes is brains she boxing.

Since Sheila and her family left, Gloria was the only best friend I have. At first she was kind of stuck up. Always skinning up she face as she see mess. Perhaps because she going to town school, she think she better than anybody. Town school children always think they better than country children. They think they brighter than them, but sometimes they dunce as bat. A few weeks after they moved in the house, she invited me to her birthday party . . . From that time, little by little we became friends. Mammy and her mother became friends too, not like Miss Chrissie, but they got on good. Gloria said I reminded her of a friend she had whose mother was funny in the head. I don't understand how one minute a person could be alright, going about their business good, looking after their family and things, then just like that they gone funny in the head. It's as if the sun burn out their brains.

145

Look at Miss Joycelyn by the big school. I never see anything like that. The Thursday she was helping out in the Catholic harvest. She had a stall selling saltfish souse and bread, with mauby and ginger beer. That was the Thursday, you know. Bright and early Friday morning, we heard a dinging coming down Cacoben Hill. Loud loud singing coming down the hill. When the person reached the foreroad I asked Mammy if I could go and see what was happening. It was holiday so I didn't have to get ready for school. By the time I reached the foreroad a big crowd was watching Miss Joycelyn preaching. She had a bible in her hand, a little black bag tied around her neck and she up and down the road preaching and singing, saying she had a message from God. From that day she got worse. Night and day she was up and down the road making noise. In the end her family signed doctor paper for her to go to Richmond Hill. I don't understand how these things happen at all. I hear in big countries like England and Canada people, especially people from the Caribbean and perhaps Africa who not accustomed to the weather, you know with all that snow and cold, they go funny quick quick. I could understand that. I say perhaps because they not accustomed to the cold, so when the snow fall on their heads for a long time it soak into their skull, even get into their blood, thin it out and that could cause the madness. Perhaps the snow even freeze the brains.

In Grenada things different; the sun always hot . . . Everything is nice and cool, you know what I mean. When I say cool I mean quiet and easy. In the rainy season everywhere green, even when the sun hot. Sometimes in the dry season the sun so hot that the tar on the road melts. You could see the heat rising from the ground as if there is a big blaze of fire underneath. During those months the earth is baked until it split in places. Still everything nice and relaxed. Nobody rushing about to burst veins in their head, so I don't understand how people go crazy. Mammy says sometimes its obeah. She say some people going about looking nice and innocent, but they don't wash their hands. I didn't understand, because some of the people I know that gone funny are very clean people. I thought was only nasty people who don't wash their hands because they 'fraid water. Mammy said when I get bigger I would understand these things. I'm sure all is not always nastiness, though. I think sometimes it runs in the blood. Perhaps it's the same with Gloria friend's mother. One day I had to ask her if she sure she and the girl that was not family from way back, because of the way she carry on sometimes. Another habit she had was, we could be together talking and laughing – then just like that she would get vex or forget that I'm with her and she would start singing. Other times she would talk and talk, not giving me a chance to say one word. When I said she and her old time friend could be family, she asked me if I think craziness run in her blood or something. She said perhaps me and her is family, but I doubted that. You could see that she has Carib blood in her, while every bone in me feel like African. Gloria said that doesn't mean we can't be family. She said her mother told her that the whole of Grenada is one family, even if not blood family, but still family.

A year after Gloria came to live in Grand Roy the Government opened a big secondary school in Gouyave Estate. The people in the Ministry of Education decided to open secondary schools in the country. They said to help the children whose parents cannot afford to send them to town school.

Experienced teacher from schools in other parishes came to make up the staff, along with some from the Anglican and Catholic schools. The Ministry of Education sort of spread the teachers around. Mr Herbert who used to teach in the Anglican school was made the headmaster. He went to England for months to train before the school opened, so when the school opened he was ready to take on the job. The children in the high standard in the ordinary schools went there. After everything settled down, teacher Herbert started giving the bright pupils in standard seven a chance to teach, sort of training them to be pupil teachers. They used to teach alongside the experienced teachers, and the same time take lessons for the pupil teachers' exams. At first, when Mammy said she was sending me to the new school from, I was vexed because I was happy where I was, but it turned out that I did not have a choice anyway. I had 13 going on 14, and the way the education ministry changed the school system I had to change school. There were three other secondary schools opened at the same time, one in Grenville, one in St. Davids and the other in Sauteurs. Gloria changed school as well. Her mother said it was easier than sending her to town school.

It was strange at first. At the old school we all knew each other, whether you in the top class or in the infants; everybody sort of knew each other family. In the new school, even some of the teachers were complete strangers. Some of the new ones were very nice, especially the men. I don't mean good looking or anything like that, but polite, friendly and very caring. I was in standard five with some children who were older than me. Some of the pupils in standard seven was supposed to be taking lessons for School Leaving Certificate Examination, but I was sure that some of them, especially some of the girls, had other exams on their minds. You could see the way they dolls up themselves to come to

148

school . . . with lipstick and powder and things like that. Mammy would half kill me if she catch me putting on lipstick to go to school.

I noticed the way some of the girls carried on. That Yvette from Coastguard was the leader. She was really pretty but a capital dunce. Everybody saying the only certificate she studying for was the one teacher Brewster will give her. Although me and Gloria was younger than these girls, we still used to hear about what went on. Then again, some of it was not really secret because apparently the headmaster heard about what went on. He gave teacher Brewster a strong lecture. What that Brewster used to do was to go to the girl house pretending he helping her with her lessons, then when her parents' back turn was something else. The man not pretty self . . . He was the ugliest teacher in the school. Eyes like crab eyes, head like bicycle seat. His legs so bow you could walk straight between his legs without bending your back, still he playing some kind of sagaboy. Teacher Bennet was the most handsome in the school, and he did not carry on as that Brewster. He was not a showoff. I hear he only came to the new school to get some more experience before going into a top job at the Ministry of Education. Everybody in the school liked him, he was so nice. I was glad he was still in the school when I reached to standard seven. By that time some of the other girls already left and that Brewster got the sack. The gossip was that Yvette was making baby, and she said was his. When her parents went to see him he was rude to them, so they not only reported to the headmaster but also went to the Minister of Education. The next thing we heard was he gone to England. Yvette so stupid telling everybody that he going to send for her when he settle down in England to get married. Send for her! She'll wait

149

till hatchet turn hammer. She too stupid, and her mother used to join her in her nonsense. People used to laugh at them behind their backs. The truth was everybody knew that Brewster was lying. He was engaged to a girl down in Spring and she already had her papers ready to go to England to meet him. Anyway, that's their business.

Time fly so fast, before you bat your eyes it's three years since our school opened. This year, teacher Herbert picked me, Henry and Sylvia to train as pupil teachers. I was studying hard. No way I letting Sylvia past exam in front me to show off. Although Gloria was not in the same class she still used to come to lessons with me. Mammy is a funny person. Always preparing in case things don't work out. She always on about how life is not a straight road; we must all prepare something else just in case. That is why she sent me in town to take commercial lessons. She says if I don't pass the teachers' exams I could find work in an office.

The new school was very good. After teacher Brewster and another woman teacher who used to run round with the boys in standard 6 left, things really improved. Teacher Herbert made everybody, teachers as well as pupils, buckle down to hard work. About the time when everybody was cautioned about their behaviour in and out of school, teacher Bennett and teacher Marion started seeing each other. It must of been very hard for them to keep it a secret. I didn't find anything wrong in the way they were always together, laughing and things. Sometimes as if is only the two of them in the place. Not that they carried on in front us, but you could see the way they looked at each other. Just by looking at them you could see there was something special between them.

One day I was standing on the stage in standard three. I saw teacher Bennett standing by standard two blackboard looking at teacher Marion. He stood there just looking at her and smiling. She was writing on her blackboard, not even knowing he was standing there looking at her. I watched him watching her. I couldn't see anything different with her, but as he watched her his face was sort of soft and loving. I didn't understnd but I felt kind of happy for them. Because of Brewster and the other teacher, I suppose they had to be extra careful. Teacher Bennett was nothing like the other one, he was a gentleman. Because he knew what people mouth was like, they talked to the headmaster about their relationship. When I heard that, I thought that was just like teacher Bennett: always have manners. That's one reason why people liked him. Not just him, teacher Marion as well – she was a real lady.

Sometimes on Sundays they would go in the bay and bathe. They don't stay where plenty was. They would either go to La Poutree or White Gate, although they had to walk a little because teacher Marion lived in Maran and teacher Brewster come from Florida. Gloria told me one night she and her mother was going home late. The moonlight was bright like daylight. She said because her mother passed by her cousin across the bridge, by the time they reached the road the late bus had already gone down so they had to walk. She said when they reached the tambranch tree by the cemetery, right by the water pipe they saw somebody sitting on the wall. At first they thought was one person but when they got closer they noticed that the man pulled his head from the woman's face. She said she made them out straight away. Gloria's mother said 'Goodnight,' and before she Gloria could open her mouth to say 'Howdy,' her mother pushed her in front her. When she said she didn't have the chance to say goodnight to the teachers, her mother told her

151

she too farse in big people business. Since they told the headmaster how things were between them they were not secretive any more, not carrying on in front people but being more together.

The day we broke up for Christmas holiday we all had a big surprise. Not me and Gloria really, because we knew what was happening long before a lot of people in the school. Anyway, that day we finished saying prayers, then the headmaster started his usual speech. He said we done very well during a very difficult twelve months and thanked us, especially the teachers for their hard work and dedication. He went on about what he expects of us during the coming year. He talked to the pupils who will be taking School Leaving exams and the pupil teachers who studying for their first exams. At the last minute, as if he forgot, but we know that that man never forgets anything, he sort of cleared his throat. We know he was only playing forget. We sometimes wonder how that little square head could hold so much things, even small things he never forgets. Even if it's three months ago a pupil did something wrong and did not get punished, don't think he has forgotten. He storing up the licks. The next time he catches that person, Lord have mercy on you. As I was saying, he was playing smart. We knew something was up. The way the teachers came to school looking as if they going somewhere special. Teacher Bennett dressed in his best suit, white shirt and spotted red and black tie. Teacher Marion looked so nice as if she going to church or something.

'Eh, em,' teacher Herbert cleared his throat again. That was his serious business, 'eh em'. We waited. We knew the different tones of his 'eh em'. If he has the old piece of leather belt swinging in his hands when he gives his serious 'eh em', we start praying. If it's a pupil in the big class that did something wrong, Lord have mercy on that person. He always preached that we are the pillars of the school, not only in the school yard but everyday and everywhere. He said that everybody is looking at us, especially the bigger girls and boys.

'Eh em!' he cleared his throat again. 'Ting ting!' He gave the bell a little touch. Just a little ting and the hall went quiet. 'Eh em'. Again he cleared his throat. He must have something in his throat, or perhaps he catching cold I thought to myself. This time he turned to teacher Bennett and teacher Marion. Gloria was standing next to me. She pinched me on my leg. I almost bawled out. We knew what the headmaster was about to say. Since the evening teacher Marion passed by us I knew. I was surprised to see them. When I saw these two people jumping the big stone under the damson tree behind Mr Magnus kitchen, I didn't think it could be teacher Marion and teacher Bennett.

'Aye aye teacher, what you doing up here?' that was Mammy. She always telling me that I see too much, but nothing pass her. 'Aaye. What a surprise! Take care, take care on that stone,' she left where she was behind the house and went in the front yard to meet them as them came into our front yard.

'Evening Ma'am,' teacher Bennett greeted Mammy.

'Evening teach. Aye aye good to see all you. How you do? You come to see Flora?' Mammy went on without giving the people time to answer.

'Evening Miss Joyce,' teacher Marion greeted my mother. 'We just passing. We going in the pasture by Miss Gracelyn.' They were standing under the hibiscus tree in the boundary.

153

'Miss Gracelyn! She sick?' Mammy was concerned. 'I must go and see her later.'

Teacher Marion laughed. 'Sick?! I don't think she ever sick in her life!'

'Oh hoye!' Mammy pammed her lips and squinted her eyes. I was leaning out of the kitchen window watching her. I know she wanted to know more.

'Is a long time I haven't seen her. I always sending message to her, but now I have to see her,' teacher Marion said. Mammy lips pammed tighter. I could see she wanted to ask question, but waiting a little.

'She is my grandmother, you know.' At last information Mammy was waiting for.

'You grandmother! Who you mean? Not Miss Gracelyn in the pasture behind the Church of God?!' Mammy sounded baffled.

'Yes Ma'am. Miss Gracelyn in the pasture is my grandmother.'

When I heard that my ears pricked up. As I said, before since I born Miss Gracelyn living in the little house in the pasture. Long before the Church of God people started praying in the house next to her. The house was really Mr Cato, but when the old man died and the boys went overseas the house stayed empty until Mano came from Trinidad saying he is preacher and started using the house for church. The place was almost broken down, but they fixed it up. Mr Cato boy, the one who said he going to Africa, the same way Boca cousin Melda said he going to find his family in Africa, came back a few years ago, he didn't mind the people using the house. All the time Miss Gracelyn living in the pasture we never hear she had grandchildren. Some people used to talk about her one son who left the island years and

154

years ago and never came back, but no body said anything about grandchildren. Now teacher Marion telling Mammy that the old lady is her grandmother.

'True, Ma'am,' teacher Bennett said. 'Miss Gracelyn is Marion grandmother.'

'But I only know Miss Gracelyn had one son!' Mammy eyebrow was sort of squeezed in and she tried to make her mouth narrow narrow. When she does that I know she is thinking. 'I remember the lady had a son they call em . . . em . . . ' she went on.

'Mayhee,' teacher finished for her. 'Mayhee, that's my father.'

'Yeh, Mayhee,' Mammy said. 'But I didn't know he had children in Grenada.' She had that 'Fancy-that' look across her face.

Teacher Marion laughed. 'My father was a knockabout when he was young,' she said. 'My mother lived in River Sally. That's where they met.'

'Oh hoye. I see!' Mammy shook her head. A smile stretched across her broad face. The way her face changed direction, her eyes dipped inside her head and the cheekbones sort of pulled to meet her nose, I knew she had something else on her mind. Heh, my mother Joyce; I know her too much.

'Aaye, so teach, all you going for the old lady blessing then?' Mammy asked, looking from one teacher to the other, bold bold in their face, no shame at all. As I said, that's Mammy. She always said if you want to know anything for sure, ask straight – don't listen to gossip.

Teacher Marion looked a bit shy. Perhaps because she saw me in the kitchen window. I said 'Afternoon,' and went inside pretending to be doing my housework. I tried to listen, but could not hear everything. When I heard Mammy laughed and said 'That's good man, really good,' I had an idea what they were talking about. After a few minutes, Mammy came in the kitchen, full up a plastic bag of things for them . . . mandarin, golden apples, a few zabucca and other little things; then they went through Miss Evelyn front yard to go down the pasture.

'Flo, Flora you doh hear?' Mammy came back to the kitchen all excited. 'You doh hear what the teachers say?'

'What?' I answered, as if I don't know what she talking about.

'What you mean . . . what! They getting married. I really glad for them. Two very nice people. Some people might run their mouth, but I know they going to make it.' The way Mammy went on you would think was her family getting married.

'When Mammy? They say when?' I was getting exciting too. 'I wonder if they going to invite anybody in the school? I mean the children like!' I said that, thinking it would be nice to be invited to a proper wedding, not just the fête.

'I don't know about all the children,' Mammy said. 'But I expect the school choir to sing at the wedding. I can't see teachers getting married and the choir not singing, not the way your headmaster like to show off so. That man and his singing is something else.'

I burst out one laugh. Mammy is right, you know. Teacher Herbert is something when come to his choir. Aye aye, you should see him when the choir practising. If mosquito biting you, you can't slap it. When he hold up that piece of stick and fix those little rat eyes on you, the little head like a roast breadfruit on a pole. When he starts, you better watch out.

156

I was thinking to myself, didn't realised that I said about his head loud for Mammy to hear, until she shouted at me.

'Flora don't be inpertinent,' she said. I don't think she was really vex, only reminding me about my manners.

'Sorry.' I said.

'They might tell the whole school before you all break up for the holiday. That would be good. Go on Christmas holiday with some good news,' Mammy added. She was right. Just what she said was how it happened.

Teacher Herbert smart. He waited for the last day to say anything. When we did everything to close school for the holiday he gave his 'serious business' clear throat.

'Eh em em,' he started again. All eyes were then on his face, although I took little glance at teacher Marion and teacher Bennett where they were standing in front the stage. 'Today we will be closing school on a very happy note,' he went on, his eyes yipping across a sea of black faces. 'Today I have a special announcement to make. No no, not just an announcement but also an invitation. A very special invitation.' I was getting a bit edgy. Why don't he say what he has to say? He always making long long speeches. One day words will get vex and turn their backs on him, I was thinking.

'Yes, a very special invitation indeed,' he turned towards the teachers standing on the stage. 'Teacher Marion and teacher Bennett told me they are getting married.'

'Woye o yoye, wedding cake and wine,' Reginald, one of the boys in standard six, shouted out. With that the school erupted. Teachers and pupils started clapping and shouting. Bang, bang, bang the hammer crashed on the headmaster's table. Bang, bang, bang.

'Quiet children,' teacher Herbert shouted. 'Quiet. Let me

finish. Our teachers are getting married and they have honoured us by asking the choir to sing at the wedding.'

I tell you, Christmas started the same time. I don't know how I reached by the stage where the teachers were standing, but the next thing I knew I was hugging teacher Marion and water running down my face. Why tears, I don't know.

'When? When is the wedding?' The children wanted to know. 'When is the wedding?' we shouted.

Teacher Bennett then went on the stage and held up his hands for attention. 'We have not set the day yet,' he said, 'but it would be after the pupil teachers' and School Leaving exams next year.'

'Aawh,' the note of disappointment came from the children. 'We thought we getting cake and wine for Christmas.' That was Reginald again.

'Don't be disappointed. I promise you a good time,' teacher Bennett said. 'Remember we have to think of our school first and our futures. Remember what the headmaster said. Next year we must be top of the Island Honours List. Top. Alright boys and girls?'

'Alright, alright,' we shouted.

'Happy Christmas, everybody,' he shouted back. With that, he and teacher Marion pushed through the crowd and left. Teacher Marion was crying.

'Ting a ling ling ting.' Teacher Herbert rang the bell. 'Boys and girls remember, remember wherever you are, eyes are on you. Remember you are the school always. Next year we have a lot to do. Remember what teacher Bennett said, Florida Secondary School must be top of the Honours List next year. We are shooting for the sky. And of course there is the wedding. Have a happy Christmas. See you all next year.'

Christmas that year was good for me and Mammy. She

got a pay rise and some back pay, and I got a little money for myself. Every holiday Mammy used to send me at Miss Maureen to learn to sew and to do fancy work. I was very good at doing fancy work. I could hand work pillowcases and towels real pretty. Mammy used to buy flour bags and wash them for me. When she washed them and bleached them they look like pure white cotton cloth. One day a woman came up by Miss Maureen and saw me working a hand towel. I did the edging in green scallop and was working on the pattern on the two corners. I was working two baskets of flowers. The basket in mattey brown, the flower stem in deep brown, the leaves in green, and the flowers red with yellow centre. The woman watched me for a long time. She said she never seen anything so pretty. She also said that she could watch me for the whole day the way I handled the needle. She ask me if I could do something for her. I was feeling good but I had to ask Miss Maureen first. She said yes. If I wanted to do it, I should do it. I couldn't wait to tell Mammy. Fancy a stranger asking me do fancy work for her! Mammy said I should do a pair of pillowcases. She was so glad you would think was Princess Margaret that asked me.

'Aye aye girl, the lady must really like your work,' Mammy said. 'I always said it's a blessing you have, to use your head to these things so neat and pretty. You have to work quick though, because I suppose she would want to take them back with her.'

'Take back? Take back where Mammy? You know the woman?'

'I don't know her, but the other day I saw her passing going up the road. She is Miss Cochrane, that living in Church Street in town, niece. She on holiday from Canada.'

'Canada!' My eyes popped out. 'Canada; you mean she might take the pillowcases to Canada?'

'Chupes', Mammy sucked her teeth. 'Aaye what you mean Canada? Girl look in the basket under the bed and see what cloth and thread you get, nuh? Did she tell you what pattern she wanted? You have to do them real nice, you.'

'Aye aye, Mammy, I know. I'll work it in plain white. Not a dull white, but a sharp, shining white. A basket of flowers, but in white cut outs. If I have the time I might do a small towel with some butterflies.'

The next morning when I went up to Miss Maureen she gave me three dollars that the Canada lady left for me to cloth and embroidery thread. Miss Maureen said she really liked my work. We have five weeks left of the August holiday so I had to work hard to try to finish them before school opened in September at least. When I said I don't think I would be able to finish it, Mammy said I too damn lazy. I really worked hard that August. My friends used to laugh at me, because when they going galavanting I'll stay home and work on the pillowcases. Lydia used to say I think I doing work for competition, but when I finished she was so envious she wanted me to show her how to do fancy work. I finished before school opened, but I was a bit sad because the woman went back to Canada before they were finished. Miss Maureen took them to post to her. I was disappointed because I wanted to see her face when she saw them. I forgot all about them once I gave them to Miss Maureen.

One evening, I think was about the second week in December when I went to the post office, Miss Lewis gave me an overseas letter addressed to me. I was surprised. I never got any overseas letter before. I looked at the handwriting, but I couldn't make it out. The stamp was a Canada stamp, but the last person I had on my mind was the woman I did the fancy work for. I ran home quick quick as anything to show Mammy. When I opened the letter the first thing that fell out was a ten-dollar note – a Canadian ten-dollar note! I looked at Mammy with my mouth opened. You should of seen her eyes; they popped out even bigger. In the letter the Canadian woman said she was really pleased with the work. She said she was showing off to her friends. She said her friends want to know where she bought them and if she could buy some for them. When she told them that I made them, they ask if she could ask me to do some for them. She said she will be coming back to Grenada the next year August and she would like me to do something for her. I felt so proud. As for Mammy, you would think it was letter from the Queen of England. She told everybody how I got a lot of money from Canada for my fancy work.

As I said that year, Christmas things was good with us. With Mammy back pay and pay rise we bought new curtains, glasses, plates and spoons. Mammy told me to save some of my money for the wedding and we can use the rest to make up for Christmas. One treat for the house was a new centre table she bought. Apart from my usual new clothes for Christmas she bought me an extra school uniform. She bought the skirt and bodice a little bit big for me, because she says I still growing.

8

Since my brother Christopher gone overseas and Janice died, is only me and Mammy living in the house. Sometimes things does be a bit bad with us, but on the whole we were not worse than anybody else. This time things were going good. Mammy always says when things going too good the devil is planning trouble. I don't know where she get her sayings from, but I learn to listen to her because there usually be some truth in them. Was as if she sees things before they happen. Just after Christmas, I believe was about the second week in January, I got a letter in the post office for Mammy. The stamp was stamped St. Croix. I didn't take any notice of it. As soon as I gave Mammy the letter she started quarrelling. She chucked it on the table and carried on quarrelling, just like that. One minute she happy sorting out her business, the next she vex vex. She was planning how we could get some money to paint over the house. Last year we broke down the kitchen from where it was and joined it on to the house, so now we don't have to go outside the house to get to the kitchen. I am already taking lessons for School Leaving exams and teacher Herbert already told me, Henry and Sylvia he would give us a chance to teach during the year. So everything was alright. Alright until

Mammy got that letter. I thought it was funny she did not open it the same time as she usually do. The way she chucked it on the table was as if she knew what was in it. She kept on quarrelling to herself. I could not make out what she was saying; the only thing I heard clearly was 'The damn man, the blasted man.'

The letter came the Friday morning. Friday night she still hadn't opened it.

'Aaye, Mammy you forget to open you letter.' She gave me one bad eye you would think was bad word I cursed.

'You too damn farse,' she snapped. 'Too damn farse. You want to know who it from. You don't see it from St. Croix. You don't see!'

Even then, nothing in my brain connected with St. Croix. When she shouted at me I noticed her eyes; they were kind of sad. She looked at me and I could see the pain across her face. My eyes began to feel wet. I don't like to see Mammy sad.

'What's the matter Mammy?' I asked. I went and put my hand around her waist. 'You look sad. Who the letter from?' Although she snapped at me a few minutes before, but I wanted to know.

'The letter from St. Croix. I think it's from your father,' she whispered through a deep sigh.

Years I haven't heard anything about my father. Years since Mammy went to that place for a little while. A few months after she came back she had Janice. Since then Janice died. Now that letter come and Mammy look so sad, and only quarrelling with herself. I hope it's not trouble. After we had our food, Mammy opened the letter. Woye o yoye! Was then she really started to quarrel.

'Whey he think he going eh? Whey! He run life in dat

place, now he full of cocobaye he talking about coming home to his wife and child. Wife and child, eh! Let him come!' Mammy was having a bacanal with herself.

'Who coming, Mammy? Not me father?' I was upset because Mammy was upset. 'When he coming? What he coming for?'

'Coming! Whey! He know whey he going. Is now people go say they didn't know I had bad mind so. After all these years he didn't want to know us. He child died, he don't drop a line to ask how I bury her. Now he talking about coming home! He so damn brass he didn't even give me a chance to answer the letter. He don't even know if the old house standing up on one post or three. He talking about he coming home. I want to know whey he think he going.'

I don't know how news travel so fast in this place. It's worse than how I hear in Africa they usually beat drums to pass news from one village to the other. Here in Grenada they don't beat drums; I think they talk to the bush. Only last night, that's Friday, Mammy opened the letter and find out 'bout my father coming, or wanting to come, home, yet Saturday morning people know already. Mammy wanted to ask Miss Marry to buy three yards of cloth in town for her and I wanted to borrow a book from James, so me and her was going round by Miss Marry when we meet Miss Chrissie. Is a long time she don't come by us to beat mouth with Mammy. The first thing Miss Chrissie asked Mammy was what she was going to do. Mammy didn't know what she was talking about.

'Do. What you mean do Miss Chrissie?' Mammy eyes squinted closer.

'Aye aye, look at you trouble nuh, Joyce.' Miss Chrissie

went on, not looking straight at Mammy. 'After all that time. All these years. I didn't know he used to write you!'

'What you talking about Miss Chrissie?' Mammy eyes poked in the woman face trying to get her to look at her. 'What you talking about?'

'How you mean what I talking about? You husband; I doh hear he coming!'

'Bonje!' That's all Mammy said at first. She took a deep breath. 'Saye saye I don't know. I don't know.' Then, as if she only realised what the other woman said, she added, 'Who tell you that? Who know he coming?'

'How you mean who tell me? Since last week I hear he coming, and when I hear Flora got the letter yesterday with the St. Croix stamp well . . . you know what people in this is.'

'You ever see trouble so, eh Miss Chrissie? You ever see that? All these years the man doh know he have family in Grenada. Now he don't have no use to anybody he talking about coming home. Coming home! Whey he going, eh, whey he going?'

'I know saye saye. I know. But is you husband. I know he treat you bad, but first thing people go say is he put ring on your finger.'

'Chupes. Ring on me finger. The ring is a blasted rope round me neck. Look Miss Chrissie, I go see you eh. I go see you.' Then she went off. I had to run to catch up with her. Miss Chrissie shook her head as if she felt sorry for us.

That whole day, all Mammy did was quarrel. Every minute she quarrelling and finding fault with people. After we did the shopping she started cleaning the house. I always helped her. While she washing I might be sweeping or something. Somehow I couldn't do anything right. Every minute she on at me. 'Flora do this'; 'Flora do that', and no matter what I did I was wrong. She just shouted at me. I did not know when my father was coming. I could not remember what he looked like, but I made up my mind that I did not like him. If he made Mammy so unhappy and he not even here, yet he can't be a nice person. Later in the evening Miss Mae Mae passed by us. Was then I heard he was coming the next week. I felt bad, real bad. Sort of left out. Usually everything is me and Mammy. All her business she would tell me. Sometimes if she wanted to do something, me and her will sit down and she'll tell me so and so. Sometimes even asking me what I think. She would even give me the money to go and buy things for the house. Like when she broke down the kitchen last year, was me that went to the timber yard and ordered the board and went to the shop for the nails and thing that the carpenter wanted.

Now my father coming, everybody knew what was going but me. When Miss Mae Mae left I started crying. I was in the kitchen washing the wares and the eye water just poured down my face. Mammy saw me crying, and asked what was wrong. At first I said 'Nothing; nothing wrong'. She said if nothing was wrong and I crying she'll give me something to cry about. Was a long time since she gave me a beating but she was in such a bad mood anything could happen.

'Mammy!' I stammered. 'Mammy, what's happening? Why you don't talk to me? Since you get the letter yesterday, you only quarrelling quarrelling and shouting at me. Me and you here good good. You not telling me anything. Now I hear you tell Miss Mae Mae that my father coming next week.' I just went on. I was not sure what I expected Mammy to do. I would not of been surprised if she gave me a beating. She was quiet. Stood in front the kitchen quiet. When I looked at her I saw water in the corner of her eyes. Then she came into the kitchen and hugged me. Hugged me tight tight.

'What's the matter, Mammy? Is true is next week my father coming? What he coming for?' I asked.

She took a deep breath. Then sort of waited for a few minutes before saying anything. Was as if she was not sure whether she should tell me anything. 'He sick.' That's all she said. 'He sick.'

'Sick!' I was vex. 'Sick! If he sick why he don't go to hospital in St. Croix? Eh; if he sick why he don't go in hospital where he living?'

'I don't know, child. I don't know. All the time he on his two foot he don't remember us. Now he cablay he talking about coming to his family.'

I was vex and afraid as well. Tears was pouring down my face. All kind of things started running through my mind. Mammy said the man had cocobaye, if is true where he going. Why he don't stay where he get the cocobaye? Eh where he don't stay dey? She said he cabblay; if is true then how he go climb on boat or plane?

Sunday the house was quiet in a funny sort of a way. I went to church but Mammy said she and God not talking to each other. I think perhaps she didn't want to talk to people in the church about my father coming. She was not quarrelling as the day before. She was not saying anything much either. Miss Chrissie passed by us when she came from church. She and Mammy sat on the step beating mouth like old times, but they were not laughing hearty laugh. When she was leaving Miss Chrissie said to Mammy 'Don't worry. God is love. He work in mysterious ways.'

Miss Chrissie saying about God work in a mysterious way

167

reminded me of the old woman who used to live in the little house behind Miss Deeka bakery. Although she died a long long time, people always remember the strange things she used to say. One I always remember was . . . 'Man point . . . man appoint.' I never understood what she meant until one day after she died Mr George explained it to me. What she really meant was man makes plans but God had already preplanned man's life span, or something like that.

Anyway, the Tuesday evening we were on the step in front the door waiting for the food to cook when Cristilyn called Mammy and tell her there is a phone call for her in the police station. Mammy left the pot on the fire and ran down the road. I ran down behind her.

Mammy put the phone to her ears, said 'Hello.' The next thing I heard she shouted 'Dead! What yo mean dead?' Then she started to bawl. I went and hugged and tried to get her to tell me what was wrong. After a few minutes she wiped her face with her frock tail and started talking in the telephone again. Afterwards she said she did not realise that she bawled out. She said when the woman on the other end of the phone said she sorry to tell her that Mr Williams is dead, inside her went all cold that's when she must have bawled out. She said although he treated us badly all those years, something in her belly sort of pulled. Apparently he knew he was dying; that's why he wanted to come home. They say he went on and on at the woman he was living with in St. Croix about wanting to go to Grenada to lay his bones to rest, that in the end she agreed that was when he wrote the letter saying he coming.

He had told the woman even if he dead before he set foot in Grenada, still send his body home. She told him yes but she did not think that was right to send a dead body to people

168

in Grenada after all these years he spend in St. Croix. She asked Mammy if she wanted the body. Mammy didn't answer her. She said she don't think it is right, and she would do her best by him and stand his funeral in St. Croix.

I know in Grenada there is bush radio but I did not know that happened between islands as well. Before you wink the eye, all over Grenada knew that my father was dead. The news that reached us was he had TB, and on top that he had a big foot. They said since he mash dirty water in front his door the foot started scratching him, it made a little sore. All how he treated it, it wouldn't dry; in the end it turned in a life sore. But in the end what killed him was not so much the sore but the TB. They said it eat out his lungs.

After the first phone call Miss Blossom called Mammy a couple of times. One time she suggested if Mammy wanted to bury her husband she would come over with the body. I'm sure different spirit guide people at different times. It must of been the good spirit that was with Mammy that time, because of the way she spoke to the person on the phone. She said she sorry he died and we did not see his face, but he suppose to make his peace with God when he was alive. If he hadn't it wouldn't matter where he is buried; his spirit won't have any peace. She said it so calm you would believe she was practising for something. Anyway he was buried in St. Croix.

To tell the truth, up to now I can't say how I felt when I heard that my father was dead. Inside me was sort of non-feeling. Mammy was sad. I found her crying at one time, but I did not feel anything. The night we got the news that he died she sat on the step a long time, quiet quiet, with her hand under her chin. People passed. She made a little talk and just sat there. Over the next few days people who hadn't

passed by us for a long time came. When cousin Mildred
came round the second time she asked Mammy if she making
prayer for the dead. Mammy was surprised. She said making
prayers for the dead body would not send him to heaven.
She said she think it would be hypocrite. After that, other
people asked the same thing. Then Nenen Beatrice asked the
same thing, saying he wanted to rest his soul in Grenada,
that's all he was asking. Mammy agreed then to hold a nine-
day prayers. She said after all is her husband, her children
father. Anyhow you look at it, family is family. During that
week, Mammy was busy preparing for the prayer meeting.
I helped her in everything, but still I not did cry. I just
couldn't cry. The night of the prayer Miss Peters came to
offer the prayers. The house was packed with people. All in
the yard. All in Miss Evelyn yard. People we hadn't seen for
years turned up to pay their respect. I think some of them
only came for the rum and rice tea, because I'm sure they
don't even know my father. Tanty May came from Paradise
with a bus load of people. Sheila's mother brought a bus
party from Birchgrove. So much people. People from Concorde, Cotton Bailey, Gouyave, Marigot, everywhere. They
said Mammy was a good woman; they come to share her
grief.

Gloria stayed near to me all through the night. Since about
six o'clock people started singing hymns. About nine o'clock
after Miss Peters read from the bible and said a few prayers
from the prayer book, everybody started singing again. I
don't know what happened after that. I don't remember
anything. All I remembered was Nenen Beatrice shouting
out the first line to the hymn 'Rock of Ages' and the others
taking it up. Afterwards Gloria told me how she was worried
about me. She said why she stayed so near to me was because

170

she noticed I was acting strange. She said my eyes were kind of wild, and at one time I was very very quiet. Then when they started singing 'Rock of Ages' I started shaking. Then just like that I started bawling. I collapsed on the floor and bawled as if I had all the eye water stored up and it was pouring out. Not only I was bawling but I was talking about everything. Everything . . . about Christopher, Janice, everything. Afterwards I fell asleep.

Mammy said she was glad she made the prayer. When she saw all the people who turned, she felt lighter in her heart. For months after I did not feel well. I was not sick with pain or anything like that, but not well inside. I tried my best at school, but I did not realise people had noticed that something was wrong. One evening teacher Bennett came to see Mammy. When I saw him in front the door I thought he was passing to go by Miss Gracelyn. When Mammy saw him she went in the front yard to say howdy.

'Aye aye, Flora, look who in the yard nuh, aye aye,' she said. 'Evening teacher Bennett. Good to see you. How teacher Marion?' That's Mammy for you, tumbling out everything at the same time. Teacher Bennett said good evening and come up the step to the front door. He and Mammy was in front the door talking. She gave him a glass of juice. I was in the back weeding under the pepper tree. I couldn't hear what they were saying, but at one time I heard Mammy called my name. Teacher Bennett did not stay long. After about fifteen minutes he called out me that he would see me at school tomorrow.

When he left I notice Mammy looking very sad. Sad like when she heard my father was dead. I wanted to ask her what was wrong, but I was a bit scared. I don't know why. We had our food and I was going to wash the wares, when she called me inside. Lawd have merci. My heard started spinning. My mind turning over and over. What did I do wrong, I wondered? I didn't think teacher Bennett would make news on me, but you never know. Mammy was leaning over the half back door facing inside, waiting. By the time I went around the house I was shaking like jello. Mammy then came and put her arms around me, hugging me tight tight. That surprised me and made me more frightened, especially as I felt her hands trembling. She said how teacher Bennett was such a nice person. He cares for all the children in the school.

'Flora!' she said in a soft soft kind of voice. 'Flora you awright?'

'Awright? What you mean Mammy?'

'I mean you not studying nothing? I mean you not studying things you not telling me about?'

'I awright Mammy, true. I not studying nothing.'

'Eh em,' she cleared her throat. 'These days you quiet quiet. Since you father dead you not the same. You studying him?' I didn't answer. Couldn't answer. A big lump blocked my throat. My eyes began to hurt as if water was forcing to come out.

'You still studying him, eh Flora? Tell Mammy. You still studying him?' Mammy asked, turning me to face her.

I shook my head. The tears that was fighting with my eyelids won. Mammy sat on the easy chair and me on the floor. It was making dusk. One one fireflies were flying about. I could see Miss David little lamp light on Boawden Hill. Sitting in the dusky room talking to Mammy, somehow I still felt alone and lost. At that moment I missed my brother and little sister very much. I also felt very angry. Why I did

172

not know. All I knew was that I wanted my brother and sister with me, and they were not there.

'You studying you father?' Mammy repeated, and then she went on about how long he left us and gone about his business. He didn't even bother with us. Not even when his child died. He didn't write a line. Was as if when he left Grenada he throw stone behind his back. How come I studying him and falling behind with my schoolwork? Then I realised why teacher Bennett came to see her.

'What you mean, Mammy? I do my schoolwork, you know.'

Mammy took a deep breath. 'Teacher Bennett think you take on you father death so bad you not concentrating as before. You father done dead and gone; you can't study him and forget yourself.'

I sat on the floor, my hands in my lap. My body tight. I wanted to say something, and at the same time I wanted to disappear like a spirit. I could feel Mammy eyes on me. I know she was waiting for me to say something.

'I not feeling too good,' I whispered.

'You have pain?'

'No Mammy. Not sick pain, but sick. I wish he came back to see us, even if for a little while. Even for once, or even asked me to come to St. Croix to spend time with him. I feel as something is wrong with me. Christopher gone overseas. Janice dead. Now my father dead without even coming back. Something must be wrong with me, why God making these things happen to people I like.'

Mammy hugged me. She rocked me like she used to do when I was younger.

'Flora,' she said. 'Don't ever let me hear that again.'

'Sorry Mammy, but that's how I feel. I don't mean some-

173

thing wrong with you. Is me. I feel perhaps jumbie following me.'

Mammy laughed. Funny woman. Serious business going on and she laughing. Wasn't hearty laugh, though. It was sort of laugh to cover eye water.

'Flora Williams, you are the most blessed person God ever made. You hear me, the most blessed.' Then she started talking about the bible and how God has a reason for things that happen. She said people would always question why and when things happen, saying this or that is not right. But God has a plan for all of us. We talked for a long time. We did not realise we were sitting in a dark house. After that I felt much better. I still think about Janice, Christopher and my father, but as Mammy said it's God work. Time was going fast. It was already February. Teacher Herbert took me on as a pupil teacher as he promised. With School Leaving exams in September and I wanted to have a go at the pupil teachers' exam in October as well, it was really hard work. On top of that, teacher Bennett and teacher Marion had set the date for the wedding. Everybody was working hard. Teacher Anna gave us extra lessons on Saturdays. Gloria was studying for the School Leaving exams, so we go to Gouyave Estate on Saturdays as well. It's like we always together. She could be very strange sometimes. She was vex with me because she wasn't in the choir practising for the wedding. It wasn't my fault she can't sing. One thing with teacher Herbert, if he feels you can't sing, no matter who it is, even his own children, he not taking you in the choir. Anyway, with all the hard work time passed quickly, and before we know it it was time to take the exams. The School Leaving papers were very easy. I didn't have any problems, but the teachers' were harder. Although I wanted to pass I didn't mind too much because teacher Herbert said that if I passed the School Leaving exams with good marks he would keep me on as a trainee pupil teacher for another year and I could take the exam the next year.

Two months after the exams was the wedding. It was to be on the Saturday before school break up for Christmas. Teacher Herbert wanted his choir to wear special clothes, like uniforms. The boys had to wear a proper suit . . . navy trousers and jacket, with white shirt and blue bow tie. The girls in blue dress, white socks and black shoe. Miss Wilma was making the dresses and Mr Noel the boys' suit. The pattern for the dresses was simple but nice. Apart from being in the choir we were like bridesmaids. As time got closer, everybody got edgy edgy. We did not want to let our teachers down. We worried for nothing. Everything we did worked out great. Teacher Herbert bought a new baton. He was so proud in front his choir you would think he was one of his children getting married. On the day of the wedding all around the church was clean and pretty, just as if Jesus was coming. It was just like Christmas.

Teacher Bennett looked like that American film, the one who was in that film 'Island in the Sun'. He was so handsome. As for teacher Marion I don't know how to describe her but to say she was like a black angel. She looked natural and not natural. I wanted to touch her. Her dress was made of brilliant white silk. The bodice had a low neck, not too low, enough to show her pearl necklace. The back and front was covered with fine granny lace and pearls. The skirt stiff with the can can reached down to her ankle, just touching her shoes which were made from the same material as the dress. It was not high heel, more like a dancer's shoe. She did not wear a veil. Instead she had a crown of little white

175

and red flowers, like a confirmation crown. The same flowers made up her bouquet.

Although they got married in the church in Black Bay instead of the main one in Gouyave, yet the church was packed. People who were invited and those who just came to watch. Even those who came to watch were dressed up. The church was decorated from the main gate right up to the altar. Miss Gracelyn, that's teacher Marion grandmother, came to the wedding. Although teacher Marion told Mammy that Miss Gracelyn was her grandmother somehow I didn't think she would turn up at the church. Well, all the time the lady living in the pasture I never know she could dress up so. When she have on her church clothes, or when she going to bus party or something, she look nice but ordinary. At the wedding she looked nice. I mean not just dressup nice but young nice. I thought her clothes came from England or America, but I heard her telling somebody that Miss Irmine in Concorde that made the dress and she fixed up the hat for herself. She was wearing a yellow polka dot dress with a little white bolero over the bodice. It fitted her so cute. Her hat was one of those wide rimmed Venezuela soft felt hat, and she spruced it up with a wide band from the dress material. She had a white hand bag and shoes. The lady looked good.

After all the preparation the wedding day was here. Everything was going smoothly. The choir was in top form. Teacher Herbert baton working you'll think he was conducting the heavenly chorus. I was right in front the altar seeing everything that went on. I was feeling good. The priest started the service with a prayer, then the choir sang 'Bind us together Lord, bind us'.

Father Bernard was conducting the main ceremony when it happened. It sounded like a hallelujah clap of thunder shattering the peacefulness of the church. The priest had finished the part where he asked 'Would you take this person', and so on and so on, then he said something else. Just as he started 'I now pronounced . . . ' he did not finished. One piercing 'O Gawd oye', then nothing. The priest stopped in mid-sentence. Everybody fidgeted. Father Bernard started again, 'I now pronounce you . . . ' again he did not finish. This time was as if all hell let loose. 'O Gawd oye papa bunjay oye have merci on me have merci.' Everybody straining their necks to see what's happening. The priest worried; you should see the way he scanning the congregation. I looked at teacher Marion. It seemed as if she was turned into a statue. I felt so sorry for her. Teacher Bennett held her hand. 'O Lawd papa bunjay oye help me. Amway becay oye have merci on me.' Miss Gracelyn kept on bawling. No other sound in the church but hers. Even the children were quiet. 'Lawd have merci I live to see my one granddaughter marrieding. I never married but my granddaughter marrieding. Mayhee not here. I doh know where he is. He don't even know he daughter marrieding. O Gawd help me, me belly hurting me so.' Miss Agnes from on the Lance left her seat and went to the woman. She took her outside. We heard her bawling going across the school pasture towards the vicarage. I felt so sorry for the teachers. Eye water was tickling behind my eyeball.

After the ceremony Miss Agnes said that Miss Gracelyn gone home. She said that the old woman said as she sit down looking at the couple on the altar she started thinking about things that happened to her in her life. She said things became like a load on her chest and the only thing she could of done was to bawl out. She told Miss Agnes to tell the couple she sorry to upset them. She will see them soon.

177

As long as I live I won't forget that day. I have never heard anything like. People really funny. One minute Miss Gracelyn sitting there following the service good good like everybody else, the next thing like the devil take over her soul.

After the wedding we went to the big house on Maran hill for the fête. The house is built in the middle of a wide pasture. There space all around to sit down or dance or whatever you wanted to do. For the wedding it was spruced up like the church. There was all kinds of foods and drinks. There were tables of food and drinks on the balcony and under the big mango tree to the side of the house, but the main table with the wedding cake was in the middle of the big room inside the house. The bride and groom were sitting at the table. People went up to talk to them every minute. There was also a steel band on the balcony. People was dancing inside the house and on the grass. Everybody was enjoying themselves. Eating, drinking and dancing. Miss Gracelyn came to the fête after all. She went home changed her clothes and came to celebrate with her granddaughter. Although the dress she had on was not as pretty as the one she wore in the church, she still looked young and nice. When she came in the house people started shooshooing and cutting eyes at her. She went inside to the bride and groom. Hugged them for a few minutes and started talkin to them. After a while we noticed teacher Marion take out a handkerchief and wiped her grandmother eyes. People so farse they wanted to know what the lady said to her family. When she finished talking to them she took up a bottle of rum from the table, sprinkled some in the corners of the room before pouring out a glass full for herself. One gulp she swallowed the rum without even a drop of water to chase it.

Teacher Marion had some of her family from River Sally to the wedding. All evening her uncle was singing, drinking and making jokes. He was sitting under the mango tree with a group of people singing calypso and dancing. After a while he took his comb out of his pocket, covered the teeth with a piece of cigarette paper, and started to blow. Although the steel band was blasting out, yet that comb music was so sweet people left the real musicians to join them. After he started, Alson took out his mouth organ and joined in. Then Joey picked up an empty bottle, started ting tinging with an old nail. Talk about music, that was better than any electric instruments. When they start playing 'I want someone to limbo with me', Cristilyn and James two standard seven pupils started limboing together. Other people were doing their own dance. When calypso music hit you, nobody cares how you dance. You just do your thing. Miss Gracelyn joined them. She made a grand entrance. Sort of cleared everybody to one side that she ended up in the middle of a semi circle. While the men played, she shilly, she shally, she shimmy and she jigged. By this time everybody stopped dancing to watch her. Mr Abraham, that's teacher Bennett godfather, joined her and it was as if they had the real African spirit in them . . . these two old people danced and danced. Their bodies moving like twenty-year-olds.

Teacher Marion uncle shouted out: 'Woye o yoye, that is fête for so.'

'Yeh,' answered Miss Gracelyn. 'Yeh, that is fête poopa.' Everybody rolled about laughing as the two old people went out of this world with the music.

When the bride and groom heard the new music, they came out. Teacher Marion looked at her grandmother and started laughing. She and teacher Bennett started dancing with the old couple, but to tell the truth they couldn't keep up. In the end they just watched. I noticed teacher Bennett looked at his wife then at the two old people, and the way he looked at his wife I'm sure something running in his mind.

Anyway, as teacher Marion uncle said, that was fête for so.